STRANDEΓ ͳ
BILLION
GRUMPY P.
BY STACY-DEANNE

Stacy-Deanne
BOOKS FOR YOUR SOUL

Readers: Thanks so much for choosing my book! I would be very appreciative if you would leave reviews when you are done. Much love!

Email: stacydeanne1@aol.com
Website: Stacy's Website [1]
Facebook: Stacy's Facebook Profile[2]
Twitter: Stacy's Twitter[3]

To receive book announcements subscribe to Stacy's mailing list:

Mailing List[4]

1. https://www.stacy-deanne.com/
2. https://www.facebook.com/stacy.deanne.5
3. https://twitter.com/stacydeanne
4. https://stacybooks.eo.page/cjjy6

CHAPTER ONE

"Aria!" Chanel Adeyami busted into her daughter's bedroom and pulled the shirtless teenage boy off of her daughter. "Richard Mosley? Aria? I can't believe this!"

"Chill, Mom." Aria reached for her wheelchair and slid into it from the bed. "Richard and I were just studying."

"Studying?" Chanel glared at Richard, who wiped Aria's lipstick off his mouth with a smirk. "You think this is funny?"

"No, ma'am." Richard grabbed his LA Rams football jersey and slipped it over his skinny brown body. "No need to get upset, Ms. Adeyami."

"Don't tell me not to get upset. You're up here in my house, in my daughter's bedroom, when I told you both that Aria is not allowed to have you in this house when I'm not here. Now that neither of you can respect my rules, you're not allowed over here at all!"

"Momma, you can't do that."

"Excuse me?" Chanel marched to Aria's chair in her patent leather heels. "This is my damn house and I can do whatever I want."

"Why are you acting like this? Richard's my boyfriend and I'm not a kid. I can have guys over here if I want."

"Oh, no you can't, Miss Thang!" Chanel followed Aria to her dresser. "Do you pay any bills around here? No. Until you do, I run this." She charged Richard who still held that grin. "And Richard, you can best believe your mother's gonna hear about this."

"Aw, man. Damn."

"Momma, stop it." Aria swerved her chair from the dresser and faced her mother. "I'm sixteen-years-old. When are you gonna stop treating me like a child?"

"When you stop acting like one. Now say goodbye to your guest because you and I need to have a talk."

"It's cool." Richard got his phone off the bed and stuffed it into his saggy jeans. "Look, I didn't wanna get Aria in any trouble, but we care about each other."

"You care about your legs?" Chanel raised an eyebrow. "If so, then you better get your little scrawny black behind out of here."

"Mom!"

"I'm counting." Chanel pointed to the doorway, tapping her foot. "One, two, three—"

"Okay, okay." Richard ran to the door. "I'll see you, Aria."

"At school and nowhere else!" Chanel yelled as he ran to the stairs. "I cannot believe you, Aria. This isn't you. Why would you purposely break my rules?"

"I wouldn't have to break them if they weren't so rigid. Mom, you never let me do anything. I'm sixteen and you treat me like I'm five."

Chanel jerked upright. "I do not."

"Yes, you do." Aria wheeled past her and back to the bed. "You won't let me go out with my friends. They all gotta come over here."

"Now wait a minute—"

"Richard is the first boyfriend you've let me have."

"I didn't *let* you have him." Chanel flipped her curly black hair off her shoulder. "You started seeing him behind my back and sneaking him in here. And you did it again today after I told you not to."

"I wouldn't have to sneak boys in if you'd let me go out on dates. At my age, kids are driving and working, but I can't go out on dates?"

Chanel sighed. She attempted to stroke her daughter's head but fearing it

would make Aria more upset, she kept her distance. "Aria, it's not that I don't want you to have a life of your own, but I don't want you making the same mistake I did."

Aria dropped her head and gripped the armrests of her chair. "You mean having me?"

"First of all, you are not a mistake. You are a gift." Chanel leaned down to her, grabbing Aria's hands. "You are the most precious gift in the world and no matter the circumstances, I wouldn't change having you."

Aria sighed.

"But I was fourteen when I got pregnant and I wouldn't wish that on anyone. I was scared and you know how my father was. Oh." Chanel rolled her eyes as she plopped down on the bed. "Strong Nigerian values, huh? No way could my father accept that his little girl had gotten knocked up by the boy down the street. But I did." She looked into Aria's eyes. "And it changed my whole life. Now I'm thirty and finally getting things on track and I want the best for you, sweetie." She stroked Aria's wide light-brown cheeks. "I don't want you to suffer or struggle. I want you to get a good education and not have so much to deal with like I did at your age."

Aria moved Chanel's hand. "You don't trust me. I'm not stupid. I'm not gonna get pregnant."

"That's the same thing I said then I got pregnant by an 18-year-old loser who didn't give a damn." Chanel sat erect. "Thought I knew everything, and I knew nothing. So dumb I thought I couldn't get pregnant the first time. Believing everything the boy told me and all he did was say stuff to get in my pants."

Aria scoffed. "You mean my father?"

"He's not your father. He's a sperm donor. The minute he found out, I was

pregnant, he enlisted in the army. He'd rather fight battles than raise his kid. Think

about that, Aria." Chanel gestured to the doorway. "Can you honestly say Richard

would be there for you if you got pregnant?"

"No offense Momma, but kids are much smarter now than they were when you were my age."

"Oh." Chanel snickered as she stood. "Oh, you think so, huh? Yeah, you know everything, don't you, Aria?"

"I could know more if you let me explore." Aria slipped back into her bed. "But you're happy keeping me here in your little bubble. I'm gonna grow up no matter what. You can't punish me because I'm in a wheelchair."

"What?" Chanel's voice cracked with agony. "What are you saying?"

"I know the deal, Ma." Aria clasped her fingers in her lap, diamond stud earrings glimmering under the lights of the ceiling fan. "If I wasn't in a chair, would you be so overprotective? You raised me with the idea that I can do whatever I want and be whoever I want, but then you wanna close me off to the rest of the world. Why?" She sniffled, eyes watering. "Why do you wanna keep me in this prison?"

Chanel held back tears. "Sweetie, I don't wanna hold you back. I—"

"You always told me that just because I'm in a chair it doesn't make me any less than anyone else, yet you treat me like I am."

"Honey, no. Oh, Aria." She went to hug her, but Aria moved back. "I love you, baby. I'm doing this for your own good."

"*My* good?" Aria wiped a tear. "Or your own?"

****

"Damn it." Wesley Babcock paced in his home office on the second floor of his 60,000 sq. ft. mansion. "This can't be right. Please tell me this is wrong, Louis."

"I'm sorry, Wes, but Babcock Electronics is tumbling in the stock market and

there seems to be no end in sight. This has been going on for a year and the investors are pulling out. Wes, we're losing millions a day."

"Fuck!" He slapped the frame picture of his parents onto the floor made of Macassar Ebony wood.

Why look at his father's condescending stare when it just reminded Wesley of how much he'd fucked up?

"I can't believe this. This company is the backbone of my family. It's my legacy, Louis. We're a staple, the most successful electronics manufacturer in the world."

"We were at least." Louis sighed. "But right now, that's living in the past. We're getting hit with a lot of outside issues. The economy, competition, scandal. You wanna hear my suggestion?"

"Not really." Wesley sat in his suede recliner, turned it toward the window, and took in the view of his majestic wonderland. His gaze settling on the waterfall that was the centerpiece of the gorgeous scene. "What is it?"

"We should think more about taking Sharon Amery up on her offer to partner up."

"No." Wesley rubbed his forehead. "I told you, we're not going into the streaming business. It has nothing to do with our brand."

"Companies have teamed up to expand their customer base for centuries, Wes. Streaming is huge. We'll still be in electronics, but we could be on top again if we paired up with Amery Inc."

"That's your answer to make things better? Jump into the overcrowded streaming market? What if that doesn't work, Louis? Then what? Jesus, next we'll be selling shoes in Walmart and opening up buffets on the corner. Absolutely not!"

"Electronics is not king like it used to be. Except for TVs, what electronics are

people buying? Every company with a brain has either started a streaming company

or has become a partner in one. That's how they stay afloat while we're drowning! Amery Inc. is the top streaming service in the world, Wesley." Louis cackled. "My God. You've been trying to avoid change all this time, but you can't. I know you wanna run this company in the same way your grandfather and your father did, but that doesn't work anymore. We need to expand and stay with the times."

"No." Wesley slammed his fist on the desk. "We're about electronics. I'm not hitching our wagon to something that might not be around in ten years."

"Babcock won't be around in *five* if we don't make a substantial change. We should close some warehouses, too. We have more inventory than we're selling. It's the main reason we're losing money. Wes, we gotta stop the bleeding! You act like you got all the time in the world to decide but you don't."

"I'm the CEO here! I decide what we do and how we do it and I am not selling out. My grandfather started this company with nothing and immediately rose to the top. That's what makes Babcock special. Now you want me to conform?" He scrunched his face. "To switch the whole purpose for why my grandfather started this company? Forget it."

"I don't want Babcock to go under! I'm not just your advisor, Wes. I'm your cousin and this company means just as much to me as it does you."

Wesley's top lip quivered. "I doubt that."

"I know you think that changing things would be a knock on you, but no one is going to think you failed, Wes."

"Really? This company has been around for decades, leading the pack and I've run it for seven years and it's failing? How do you think that makes me look to all those fuckers out there who are just waiting for me to crumble? I'm one of the richest

men in the world and I got a lot of enemies. I won't show my hand."

"So what? You'd rather risk Babcock going under just to protect your pride?"

"I'm saying we live by our business model and we die by it. I ain't changing a

damn thing. I believe in this vision."

Louis moaned. "Look, there might still be some other things I can come up with."

Wesley stroked his clean-shaven chin. "You do that because your other option is crap."

"You sound stressed."

Wesley rolled his eyes. "You think?"

"Memorial Day weekend's coming up. Why don't you go to The Village?"

"The Village?"

"Uh, yeah, the luxury resort you own?" Louis laughed. "It's been so long since you been there you've forgotten."

"You expect me to drop everything and go on a trip? I can't go gallivanting off with the mess the company is in."

"Didn't you just finish telling me you're the CEO? You can do whatever you want. Plus, the company's gonna be closed anyway for the holiday and everyone will be gone, so we won't be handling business, anyway."

"I don't know, man." Wesley leaned his head back in the chair and let out a throaty sigh. "I just don't think going off to a resort is what I need right now."

"Wes, that's exactly what you need."

CHAPTER TWO

Chanel heard Aria exiting the ramp and heading for the kitchen just as she stirred the block of cheddar cheese into the homemade macaroni. "Hey, Honey."

"Hey." Aria stopped at the island and propped her elbows on the marble countertop, pouting like she used to when she was a kid. "I'm sorry for how I acted earlier. You were right. Richard and I were wrong, and I betrayed your trust. It won't happen again."

Chanel turned from the stove, smiling. "I accept your apology, but there's something about Richard I can't put my finger on. You gotta be careful about guys like him. He's too smooth for his age."

"Mom, I'm paralyzed, but I'm not stupid."

"Of course not. Why would you say *that*?"

Aria shrugged. "It's how you make me feel."

"You think I'm overprotective because you're disabled and that's not the case." Chanel approached the island. "I'd be this crazy about you and boys, no matter what."

Aria snickered, and Chanel reached over and pinched her cheek.

"That's that smile from my beautiful little baby."

Aria giggled. "Dinner smells nice. Mac and cheese, huh?"

"Yep." Chanel dashed back to the stove. "Pork chops, mac and cheese and green beans."

"Ah, someone feeling guilty?" Aria went to the fridge and got a can of her favorite cherry soda. "Joya's coming over later. We're gonna study. Oh!" She sipped her drink. "I cannot wait until next week is over and then we have three days off for Memorial Day weekend."

"Uh, Honey?" Chanel caught Aria before she left the kitchen. "I have a surprise.

I was gonna tell you earlier, but I got sidetracked with Richard and all."

"What's going on?"

9

"It's something good, so don't be looking so suspicious." Chanel got her phone from the table. "I made plans for us to spend Memorial Day weekend together at The Village."

Aria batted her long eyelashes. "You did what?"

"We're going to the Village," Chanel squealed. "You know, the resort?"

"You mean that ritzy one your rich, mean ass boss owns?"

"Stop it."

"He's a jerk and you know it. He treats you like crap."

No matter what Chanel did, she couldn't get a break from thinking about Wesley Babcock and all the bullshit she'd taken from him in just a year of being one of his chief accountants. "Yes, he is a jerk, but all Babcock Electronics employees get fifty percent off when they visit The Village and you know there's no way in hell we'd be able to afford to go without it."

Aria scrunched her face. "You *wanna* go there?"

"Yeah, don't you?"

"Not really."

"Girl, please. Look at this place." Chanel rushed to her and pulled the website

up on her phone. "How can you resist three days at this palace in sunny El Mina, California? Just an hour away?"

Aria groaned. "Momma—"

"Hush and just look at this." Chanel strolled through the pictures. "So much we can do. There's a spa. A pool. You like to swim. Sports. They go on guided hikes in the woods and dance classes. Zip lining. Guests stay in their own cabins. Look at these beautiful cabins, Aria. This place is remarkable."

"I have plans. Joya and I wanna hang out and chill. But you can go."

Chanel blocked her from leaving. "The point of this trip is that we hardly see each other anymore. I'm always working overtime for Babcock, and you're studying or on the phone with Joya all night."

"Mom, we can't be around each other every minute."

"Yeah, but I'd like *one* minute. Come on, Aria." Chanel flicked Aria's chin. "Don't you remember the mother-daughter trips we used to take? Didn't you enjoy that? We haven't taken a trip in a while and who knows when I will get another vacation? Lord knows Wesley works me like the new girl at the DMV."

"I wanna hang with Joya."

"Aria, this place is beautiful." Chanel showed her the pics again. "Come on, honey."

"I bet they'll be no one there my age."

"Course there will be!" Chanel gushed. "They'll be teenagers all over the place."

"Not any who'd wanna hang with *me*." Aria straightened her chair. "They'll probably all be rich, Beverly Hill creeps who, if they talked to me, would only feel pity because I'm in a wheelchair."

"Stop it." Chanel pulled on Aria's long, curly ponytail. She definitely had her mother's hair. "Anyone would love being your friend."

"You wouldn't be wanting me to go to this place to get my mind off Richard?"

Chanel stuck out her lips as she went back to the stove. "Whatever gave you that idea?"

Aria crossed her arms, smirking.

"Okay, maybe part of it is I don't want him sneaking back over here or you

sneaking off to see him, but I want us to spend time together."

"I'd love to spend time with you, but it's not fair to spring this on me at the spur of the moment. You didn't even ask me if I have plans of my own. Didn't we just discuss this upstairs? Stop treating me like some little kid. I don't wanna go, okay?"

Chanel pouted, her lip drooping. "Fine." She turned back around, haphazardly stirring the mac and cheese.

Aria sighed. "Are you okay?"

"My daughter doesn't wanna spend any time with me." Chanel shrugged. "Why wouldn't I be okay?"

Aria exhaled. "Does it mean that much to you?"

Chanel looked at her over her shoulder.

"*Okay.*" Aria groaned. "I'll go."

Chanel jumped in place. "You *will*?"

"Yes." Aria rolled her eyes.

"Oh, I love you, Sweetie!" Chanel pounced on Aria and smothered her with kisses. "You're gonna have the time of your life."

"Just remember..." Aria pointed at her. "You owe me one."

****

Saturday (A Week Later)

Chanel drove through the enormous valley going on and on about how wonderful the weekend would be and how this would get her and Aria back on track.

The main reason Aria wasn't looking forward to this was because she hated always being the "one in the wheelchair." So she'd have to fake smiles as people stared and whispered, trying to guess why she was in a chair.

She sighed, sitting back in the cloth seat of her mother's Volkswagen GTI,

awaiting once again to be thrown into the fire.

"What's wrong?" Chanel drove with one hand. "You've been quiet. And another thing, you're not gonna be on that phone all weekend. Put it away."

"And waste your money? Don't you pay for the phone so I can use it?"

Chanel pushed up her orange-tinted sunglasses. "You're not gonna be talking about me with Joya behind my back the whole time. Put it up."

Groaning, Aria tucked the phone into the side pocket of her purse and laid her head on the window.

"Honey, what is it?" Chanel rubbed Aria's knee, which Aria couldn't feel, anyway. "You look sad and this is supposed to be a joyous vacation! Ha, ha! Think of all the fun you're gonna have."

"With me not being able to do half the stuff? I can't go hiking if the trail is too

rough for my chair." She stroked her ponytail. "Can't go zip lining or bungee

jumping."

"What? Sure you can." Chanel looked back and forth at her. "You can do all that stuff. Why are you talking like this? This isn't you. Aria, you're the first one to say you can do anything and you always prove you can."

She rolled her eyes.

"And even if you can't do everything, there's still plenty you *can* do. You're a great athlete and can play any sport."

Aria smiled at the praise.

"You're a heck of a dancer too." Chanel chuckled. "You dance better in your chair than some men I've dated."

They laughed.

"Why are you being so down on yourself? Did something happen?"

Aria's stomach twisted with apprehension as the luxurious welcome sign of

The Village came into view.

"Come on," Chanel said. "You know you can tell me anything."

"Richard's an asshole."

"Watch your mouth. What did he do?"

"He cheated on me, Momma."

"What?"

"After all I did for him." Aria clenched her purse. "I think he was using me."

"For what?"

Aria avoided eye contact.

"Aria..." Chanel squinted. "What did you do?"

"I helped him with his history essay."

"Okay, that doesn't sound too bad."

Aria propped her elbow against the window and laid her head in her palm.

"Something tells me there's more to the story."

"I wrote the *whole* essay for him." Aria looked Chanel in the eyes. "Now I

think he was only using me, so I'd do it."

"Wait, a minute." Chanel stopped on the side of the road. "I didn't just hear what I think I did. You wrote another student's paper for them? How could you do something like that?"

"I know it was dumb, but I really liked him and let's be honest, I don't have tons of options."

"First off, that's a load of crap. You can have any guy you want and they'd be lucky to have you. You're beautiful, you're smart, you're funny—"

"And in a chair, Mom. Look, a lot of guys like me, but they won't approach me because the situation is too uncomfortable. You know how people are. All they see is the chair. That's all I am to them."

"No." Chanel shook her head. "No, you are way more than that and you don't have to sellout your ethics for some guy. See, this is what I'm talking about. You're doing the same thing I did at your age. Aria, men are a dime a dozen. You don't need to be sacrificing your life for them."

"Not surprised to hear *you* say that." Aria crossed her arms. "Seeing as how you haven't had a boyfriend since I was thirteen."

"You say that like it's a bad thing, but it proves a woman doesn't need a man."

"Mom, please. You're just scared to fall in love because you've had bad encounters with men, but not all men are bad. And sure, it's not right for me to cheat for a guy and I knew better." Aria raised her hand. "It won't happen again, but what you're doing isn't healthy, Mom. You're throwing yourself into your work so you have an excuse not to see a guy."

"Really, Miss Thang? So I can't just be happy with my life? A woman always has to be hanging off a man's arm?"

"Of course not, but are you happy, Momma?"

"Yes." She pinched Aria's cheek. "All I need is you."

"That's not true. You need love that I can't give you."

Chanel sighed, facing ahead.

"Momma, I hear you when you're talking to Aunt Di on the phone and you say how lonely you are. How you're tired of kissing frogs and wish your Prince Charming would come along. Well, just like you say I'm a great person, so are you, but you're too busy worrying about me to run your own life."

"Wait, wait, wait. When did this get to be about *me* when this was about you

forging papers for Richard?"

"It's about us both." Aria slouched in her seat. "I just want you to be happy because I love you, Mom."

Chanel smiled. "I am happy."

"You don't miss men? Don't want someone your own age outside of Aunt Di to hang out with? Don't miss a man's touch or kiss?"

"What do you know about a man's touch or kiss?" She grimaced. "Did you sleep with Richard? Aria?"

"No."

"But if I hadn't come in that room, you would've?"

"Maybe." She squirmed. "But he's a jerk and I want nothing to do with him anymore. You should be happy."

"I'm never happy that you got hurt." Chanel rubbed Aria's cheek. "I never want that. Come on." She started the car again and got back on the road. "Let's erase this negativity. Start fresh and have some fun."

CHAPTER THREE

One look at The Village and Aria felt like she was on another planet. This certainly wasn't her normal habitat.

A picturesque sanctuary engulfed by the sun's magnificent rays and the first thing Aria noticed was no ramp, which pissed the hell out of her, but she knew it had to be around there somewhere.

In the middle of the real-life painting sat the humongous, multi-level building, which stretched as far as Aria could see. Even farther. Elegant ceramic tile ran past the sidewalks and drew your eyes to the glass double-doors. Palm trees danced in the warm breeze, not a bug in sight.

The aroma of nature mixed with Chanel's peachy perfume added ambiance to the scene full of glamourous men and women who looked like they belonged on the *Dynasty* reboot. The men with perfect shirtless abs that they couldn't wait to show off and women wearing Daisy Dukes over their bikini bottoms, but hiding nothing else.

"This place is... wow," Chanel drove toward the building with her mouth wide open. "It looks even better than on the website. You can smell the millions in the air."

"Along with the snobbishness and the fact that we stick out like a sore thumb?"

"Lighten up and enjoy being in a place we couldn't afford in our wildest dreams."

The people got more and more glamorous, looking like extras in an episode of *Beverly Hills 90210*. Perfect people in a perfect space.

Chanel parked, giggling. "Ooh, I'm so excited! We're gonna have so much fun
and leave our troubles in Sacramento."

"They have no ramp." Aria pointed toward the front.

"Huh?" Chanel grimaced as she looked. "They have to because it's against the law not to. I'll ask when I go in."

"It should be in the front."

"Don't worry, I'll find out why it's not and give them the business."

Aria chuckled but quieted down when she heard boisterous laughter and shouting coming from over the fence. "That must be where the pool's at." She perked up. If there was something she loved, it was swimming. "Yep, that definitely sounds like the pool. Come on." She opened the door. "Get my chair so I can check it out."

"Uh." Chanel jumped out the car. "I don't think you should go swimming yet. Let me check out the place."

"Mom, I'm not twelve. Jesus." Aria unhooked her seatbelt. "I'm not gonna swim, anyway. I wanna check out the people."

"You mean the *guys*." Chanel held her waist, raising her eyebrow. "For a girl who claims I don't allow her to go out with boys, you sure are boy crazy."

"Maybe if you weren't so strict I wouldn't be." Aria teasingly stuck her tongue out at her. "I'll go check things out and you check us in. Hurry."

Chanel grinned, got the wheelchair out the back, and set it up in front of Aria. "Your Highness."

Aria got into it and flew onto the sidewalk.

"Aria!"

"Yeah?" She kept going, turning her wheels at high-speed.

"I'll call you when I have the cabin number, okay?"

"Okay, Mom!" She waved.

"Be careful!"

Aria got to the fence just as a group of shirtless hotties in swim trunks
exited.

And they were looking mighty delicious.

"Oh, hey." The blond guy in the red shorts with the diamond stud earring smiled, holding the door for her. "You need some help?"

"No thanks." Aria rode through the fence. "I've been in this chair for sixteen years. I think I got it."

The guys grimaced and walked on.

She didn't mean to be sarcastic, but she got sick of people always offering help as if she were some invalid.

The scene at the pool wasn't too different from the community pool in her neighborhood except Chanel was right. You could definitely smell the money in the air. A diverse crowd of mostly teens and young adults played in the water while others lounged around, giving the resort staff orders as if they owned the world. And as always, everyone Aria passed seem to stop and stare at the girl in the wheelchair. You'd think she'd be used to it by now, but it still got under her skin.

In the grass, another group of shirtless hunks caught Aria's eye as they played volleyball with a couple of big-boobed girls who looked like they spent every moment they had under the knife.

At that age.

Aria loved volleyball, so she strolled up to them, humorously waiting for their reactions. "May I join you?"

The brunette guy in the blue swim trunks turned around and, of course, his mouth fell open when he saw Aria.

He looked like a hunky surfer boy you'd see on those teen CW soap operas. He was at least 6'4" with a body like a God.

Toned and tanned, six–pack abs and muscles only in places they needed to be, so he was slim but looked like he could've bench-pressed Aria while she was in her wheelchair.

"Uh." He blushed with boyish flirtation, until his stare fell to her wheelchair. "Uh, sure, you can join."

His friends fidgeted with sympathetic smiles.

"You play ball, huh?" Cute Boy asked.

"Uh, yes." Aria smiled. "I play volleyball, tennis and softball."

The guy with the shades on his head snickered. "You play softball and tennis?"

"Don't be an ass, Dirk," the blonde girl said. "Course she can play. People in wheelchairs play sports, moron." She smiled at Aria. "I'm Farrah and you are?"

"Aria Adeyami."

Cute Boy's coy lips set into a sincere smile, absent of arrogance, which said more than his friends. "That's a beautiful name."

"Adeyami?" The chubbier Hispanic guy snickered. "I never heard that before."

"It's Nigerian." Aria smiled at Cute Boy, who hadn't averted his cinnamon-brown eyes from her once. "My father is Nigerian."

"Like I said..." Cute Boy's silky smooth voice rolled off his tongue. "It's a beautiful name and you wear it well."

Aria tucked in her grin, her stomach tickling from the butterflies.

"I'm Alex," Cute Boy said, and then pointed to his friends and named them.

"You've met Farrah."

She waved at Aria.

"This is Dirk." Alex gestured to the pale guy with the shades and freckles. "And Miguel."

Miguel waved. "What's up?"

"Nice to meet you all." Aria smiled.

"Good, you came along because we could actually use another person." Alex tossed the ball between his hands, smiling. "Show us what you got." He handed Aria the ball, and she lobbed it sky high over the net.

"Whoa," Dirk said. "Man, that's pretty good."

"Yeah, that was great." Farrah gushed. "You could be on my team anytime."

Alex smirked at Aria, his blue trunks leaving nothing to her imagination. "Mine too."

Aria grinned. "Come on, let's play."

****

"Mr. Babcock should be ashamed! Absolutely ashamed!" Chanel carried on at the check-in counter while the poor employees behind the desk shivered as if she were holding them at gunpoint. "I know he's an ass, but didn't know he was *this* terrible. How could this place not have a ramp? How?"

"We have ramps, Ma'am," the pudgy redhead spoke as if she were afraid Chanel would strike her down. "One is in the back and the other by the spa."

"Really?" Chanel scoffed, balling her fists so she wouldn't throw anything. "So my daughter has to enter through the back like she's a second-class citizen? Ramps should be visible in the front! Duh. That's the idea of being accessible!" She slapped the porcelain counter. "This is unacceptable, and I'm reporting this place to the state for violations of the law. I will *not* let you get away with treating disabled people like an afterthought—"

"What's going on here?" a male voice boomed throughout the waiting area.

Recognizing her boss' icy tone, Chanel held her breath as she turned to face him.

The debonair Wesley Babcock strutted toward the counter and everyone rushed out of his path. He always wore suits of dark-blues or blacks, so it surprised Chanel to see him without a blazer but still wearing his button-down white shirt and those diamond cufflinks with his initials engraved in them.

In this heat.

Chanel could do nothing but chuckle. It wasn't bad enough she had to see this man everyday now he was here the one time she took a vacation.

"Ah, Miss Adeyami." Wesley flashed a sarcastic smile that belonged on magazine covers. "What a surprise to see you here, causing a scene as always. Could you try to act like a lady, please?"

She scoffed. "Excuse me?"

"You're my employee." He flexed his triangular jaws. "Which means you represent me and my company at all times and I will not have you embarrassing my brand in *my* establishment."

"Well, if you don't wanna be embarrassed in your own establishment, then you should've had a ramp in the front of your place!" She pointed to the glass doors. "Or are people in wheelchairs not allowed here?"

He grimaced, his dashing greenish-brown eyes set in a carnal stare that reminded her of a shady salesman. "What the hell are you talking about?"

"Mr. Babcock, sir." The feminine male employee dashed from behind the
counter. "It's really nothing to bother yourself with."

"The hell it's not. It's his place." Chanel held her waist. "How come there isn't a
ramp at the front entrance? That's illegal."

"Perhaps you should brush up on California laws, Miss Adeyami, or else learn
how to comprehend them better." Wesley straightened himself, shoulders squared. "The law is that we have ramps that fit the code and we do. We do not have to have them at all entrances or exits."

"But that makes no sense. My daughter has to wheel herself all the way to the back of the place to get inside? Like she's the help sneaking in or something?"

He relaxed his face, his dimples firm in his cheeks despite not smiling. "Your daughter's in a wheelchair?"

"Yes and boss or no boss, I won't let you get away with this."

He shrugged. "What are you gonna do about it?"

I'm gonna report you to the authorities!"

Wesley belted out a hefty laugh. "Honey, I practically own the authorities. You forget who you're talking to? We're up to code so you'd be wasting your time. There are ramps on all the cabins so she'll be fine—"

"That's not the point. Not having a ramp at *all* entrances, especially the main one, is disrespectful, but why should I be surprised coming from you? You don't think about anyone but yourself."

He squinted. "Miss Adeyami, I'll warn you to be quiet before you say something you'll regret."

"I won't regret it!" She stood tall. Yes, Wesley Babcock was her boss, but after a year of working with him and his selfish, horrible attitude, she'd had enough. She loved being an accountant at his company, but she couldn't take more of his crap. "You're gonna learn that you and your money aren't above the law, Mr. Babcock. Now I've put up with a lot from you—"

"And you'll put up with even more if you want a job. Now stand down and remember who you are talking to."

"Don't talk to me like that. Go to hell!"

Everyone gasped.

Chanel looked around at them, nodding. "Yeah, I said it. Everyone is so afraid of Wesley Babcock, but I'm not." She stuck her finger in his face. "You're going down for this."

"Your daughter doesn't belong here, anyway."

Chanel gasped. "*What?*"

"You heard me. This is a resort where you hike, dance, and swim and obviously she can't do neither so—"

"You bastard!" She slapped him so hard her hand stung. It took a moment to realize what she'd done and the magnitude of hell that might follow because of it, but Aria was her baby and no one, not even Wesley Babcock, could disrespect her and get away with it. "How dare you talk about my daughter that way?"

"You're fired!" He pointed to the doors. "Get the hell out of my resort and Tuesday morning, I want you to get your shit from the job and be gone forever!"

"You can fire me all you want, but you can't kick me off the resort because I paid and I have every right to be here."

He bent down, sticking his face in hers. "Says who?"

"Says company policy and even *you* can't do anything about it. I was an employee when I walked in here and I have every right to fulfill my discount and finish my trip."

"You're throwing the policy at *me*, lady?" He stuck out his chest. "I *am* the freaking policy! Get out and take your daughter with you."

"Kick me out and this will be on every news station from California to Texas." Chanel wiggled her neck. "And if you think this won't go viral, you're crazy. After all the recent scandals Babcock's been through, do you want to add another one? Huh?" She crossed her arms. "It wouldn't look good that you threw out your *single*-mother employee because she was fighting for the rights of the disabled."

Wesley groaned, rocking left and right.

"I'll be gone when the holiday weekend is over, but until then my daughter and I are gonna enjoy ourselves." Chanel slapped the counter and ordered the redhead, "Give me my damn key so I can get to my cabin."

"Uh... yes, Ma'am." The redhead took a keycard from the drawer. "Your cabin is twelve, Ma'am. Hope you enjoy your stay."

Chanel yanked the keycard and glared at Wesley. "And I'm still reporting you." She sashayed toward the doors.

"Get the hell out of here," Wesley barked. "And if you think you're getting a reference from me, you're crazier than you think!"

CHAPTER FOUR

With her hand still stinging from slapping Wesley, Chanel pushed her keycard into the door of cabin 12 and unlocked it. It seemed much bigger than the website's description and looked more like an apartment than a one-story hut with a couple of rooms.

Rustic and cozy, it made you feel at home with little effort. Don't get it twisted. They called it a "cabin" but it was an upscale space with a lengthy hallway, enormous bedrooms, and a luxurious kitchen fit for Martha Stewart to have a party in.

The reddish-brown logged walls closed in on you, bringing security and comfort.

And that deck.

Chanel walked out onto it.

Wow. It looked big enough to park a car on. She'd dreamed of having a home with a giant deck and this one stretched out toward the lake. Rambunctious guests swam, drove jet skis as if they wanted to die, and caused chaos in the warm waters by racing motorboats. Spoiled, posh millennials who probably had lifelong passes to this paradise thanks to their wealthy and snobbish parents, acted as if they owned the place.

Chanel sat on the large wooden lounge chair. The millennials' overzealous hooting and hollering was just another sign of their arrogance, but she'd deal with the noise if it meant spending three days in this magnificent place.

Just as she got used to the idea of partaking in every activity she could, Wesley Babcock popped into her head. That inky-black hair, those gallant cheek bones and all the charm and charisma possible.

He was the biggest asshole she'd ever known. They had brought her on at Babcock Electronics' a year ago to get the books in order, and she did that and then some. But her accountant duties spilled off into being Wesley's assistant. Getting his coffee. Booking his flights.

Planning his parties. Working late hours on the spur of the moment. Being constantly on call and dropping plans whenever he needed her, no matter the time of day.

Hell, she was practically the man's wife!

And yes, a strong independent woman like herself, she still put up with it. Because in just one year of working at Babcock, she'd realized her purpose. She'd found the place where she belonged. Sure, she hated Wesley, but she loved her job. She loved the employees, and it flattered her Wesley trusted her with one of the most important responsibilities.

Chanel was the backbone of operations now. She handled the expenses. She kept them on track, not even a penny left or arrived at Babcock without her knowing about it. It said a lot that Wesley trusted her because he didn't trust just anyone with the company's money.

Chanel worked her ass off for that man. Giving him all she could give and what did Chanel get? Not a raise. No extra vacations. Wesley wouldn't even let her off early one day when Aria needed to go to the doctor because she was in pain.

Chanel rocked.

No, all Chanel got was his bitching. His complaints when she made a mistake. Him questioning her decisions, even though she knew more about balancing the books than he ever would.

Never a "thank you" or "good job" in twelve months. So if he wanted to fire her,

fine. She'd hate to leave the place, but at least she wouldn't be Wesley Babcock's

punching bag anymore.

No matter how attracted she was to him. Or how her stomach tingled every time he looked at her with those passionate gazes. No matter how much she'd dreamt of him, wondered what he looked like naked, wished just once she could kiss his lips.

"Damn." She gripped her head. "Whatever happens, get that crazy thought out of your head, Chanel. Wesley Babcock is *definitely* not the one."

****

As soon as Chanel left the front desk, Wesley called down the resort manager and ordered her to set up a time for renovations for an entrance ramp, then headed to his cabin, grumbling and mumbling as two concierges followed him around like lapdogs.

The frightened young men took all of Wesley's bags to the Grand Cabin and left so fast he didn't have time to throw them out like he normally would.

Of course, the Grand Cabin was in a world of its own. It was a three-floor cabin made from the finest European wood, light fixtures and lamp posts made of pure gold, and even a state-of-the-art alarm system. It had hallways of multiple rooms full of sophisticated rustic furniture that cost more than most people's homes.

"Damn that woman." Wesley unbuttoned his shirt, revealing the sweatier T-shirt underneath as he thought about the blow-up with Chanel. If you looked up the word "bitch" in the dictionary... well, you know the rest.

"That woman!" Wesley sat on the sectional made of pure leather and African Blackwood. "Who does she think she is?" Unable to control his temper, Wesley made a quick call to Louis. "She's driving me crazy!"

Louis laughed.

"It's not funny. The woman is insane, but she crossed the line this time. I fired her ass."

"What? Wes, she's the best accountant you've ever had and you couldn't ask for a more efficient worker. She does the books like a genius and she pinpoints problems

accountants who've been working twice as long as her can't see."

"She's not gonna talk to me like some bum on the street. I am her boss, but she doesn't respect me at all."

"Maybe because you don't respect *her* or at least you don't wanna show it." Louis snickered. "Along with something else you don't wanna show."

Wesley exhaled through his nostrils, sensing where Louis was going with the conversation. "What are you talking about?"

"I know you better than anyone. This tyrannical façade you put on with everyone is the shield you hide behind so people won't get close to you."

"Ah, this again?" Wesley rested his long arm on the back of the sofa. "I don't need an armchair shrink."

"You need something because it amazes me how much Chanel frightens you."

"Frightens me?" He guffawed. "I'm not afraid of Chanel, and I don't need her bull."

"No, she's someone you need very much." Louis sighed. "And that scares you to death because you hate having to depend on anyone but yourself. Always have. You've never been able to be vulnerable with anyone, so Chanel's a threat to you."

"That's ridiculous."

"Look at how crazy she gets you all the time. You've gone toe-to-toe with some of the biggest tyrants in the business world and had them running away like kittens, yet you can't tell Chanel you love her?"

Words sputtered from Wesley's mouth, "L... Louis, you've obviously been

dipping into the whiskey today. Have you lost your mind? I love Chanel Adeyami?" He guffawed. "My advice, keep your job at Babcock and please don't go into therapy because you suck at it."

"Makes sense to me. She's the only woman you ever spend time with. All those late nights at the office—"

"Working. We were *working*, Louis. This is nonsense."

"Yet you don't work that closely with anyone else. Even went out to dinner with her."

"We did *not* go out to dinner." Wesley scrunched his face. "We finished

late and I bought her something to take home with her. That's completely different."

"And I've never, ever seen a woman get to you like Chanel does. She pushes your buttons and challenges you and we both know no one challenges Wesley Babcock. You're telling me that doesn't turn you on?"

When Chanel first strutted into his office after getting the job at Babcock, Wesley knew she'd be a force to reckon with. He remembered how hard it was to keep his mind on their first meeting because he couldn't ignore the sparkle in her brown eyes and those long "when are you gonna kiss me" eyelashes.

She didn't walk. She glided, reminding him of a sexy cabaret singer from Old Hollywood. With skin like melted, toasted-butterscotch ice cream, Chanel was the only person besides Louis who dared talk to Wesley above a whisper and who told him like it was whether or not he liked it.

He groaned, his middle throbbing at the thought of her full, heart-shaped lips and velvety voice.

The things he didn't like about Chanel had made her his obsession. Of course,

he couldn't risk his pride and tell her that. No way. If he did, she'd have the upper

hand and take advantage.

One thing his father had always taught him was to never be vulnerable with anyone.

Especially women.

"I'm not gonna waste time arguing with you over silly theories, Louis. I am not in love with Chanel and never could I be. The woman is insufferable and again, she's fired now, so what difference does it make? I'll have to find a new accountant now. Shit."

"Yeah, why put more on the table when we are dealing with this other mess already? Then you gotta bring in another person who has to win your trust. You were out of line, Wes. Give her the job back."

"I will not. Besides, you know how she is. Chanel wouldn't take it back."

"She'll take it back if you grovel."

"Well, that sure as hell ain't happening." Wesley took off his shirt, wincing at how musty he'd gotten in just an hour of being in the strangling heat. "Damn, I smell like a skunk. I need to get in the shower. Look, I don't wanna think about Chanel for the rest of the weekend."

"Pretty hard to do with her right there with you, huh?"

"This place is gigantic. We can avoid each other. You said I needed to relax and have fun." Wesley stood, gathering his shirt. "That's what I plan to do. Hell, I own the place. If anyone should enjoy it, it's *me*."

****

Sunday

Wesley loved to cut loose. He always had fun at The Village even though he didn't go as much as he liked.

He signed up for one of his favorite activities: the scavenger hunt. It was when

you went out into the woods with a partner, and searched for whatever item was missing and the team that found it, won. You didn't get a reward or money. The prize was the fun you had on the hunt.

Wesley loved it because, though he owned the place, the hunt always made him learn something new about the property.

Rearing to go in his hiking boots, T-shirt and Nylon travel pants, Wesley walked through the smooth trail and came to the clearing. One of the wilderness guides, Jenna, with a body that would make a priest turn his back on God, stood on the large rock in front of the group, explaining the rules of the hunt, which Wesley knew by heart.

The small group of men and women watched him in awe, perhaps intimidated to be around the man who owned the place. Some woman with an amazing ass was bending over in hiking shorts, digging in her satchel. It wasn't until she leaned up and he saw who she was that Wesley cursed Louis for suggesting he come to the resort in the first place.

Yep, Miss Adeyami.

"Oh, Jeez." Wesley groaned, rolling his eyes to the top of his head.

"Great." Chanel opened her water bottle. "Thought I had the perfect plan to stay away from you."

He tried with all his strength to ignore how luscious her tits looked in that tank top. "Had I'd known you'd be doing the hunt, I'd have gone on the cave tour instead."

She sipped. "And had I known you'd be here, I'd have dropped dead."

"No need to hurry, Darling." He snickered, looking ahead at Jenna. "I'm sure you'll be in hell soon enough."

Chanel groaned.

"Remember to have fun!" Jenna jumped off the rock, boobs jiggling in her spandex tank.

Wesley hadn't counted on so much delicious boobage.

"Now this is a team challenge." Jenna slapped her hands together with an

enthusiastic smile. "So you're each going to come up here and pull a colored ribbon from the box. The two people who have the same color are a team. Step right up."

Wesley and Chanel inched their way up the line behind everyone else.

"I sure as hell better not get the same color you get," Chanel said.

Wesley skipped three people in the line and hurriedly grabbed the green ribbon. He went back to his spot, praying to God Chanel got another color.

Or at least that's what he wanted her to think.

Being the last one up, Chanel grabbed the last ribbon. "Oh, no." She held up the green one.

"Looks like we got our teams!" Jenna laughed. "Everyone get with your partners. Chanel, you'll be with Mr. Babcock himself."

"Oh joy," she grumbled, walking back to Wesley.

"Remember," Jenna said. "You're looking for the little piggy bank. The hunt will go on until someone finds the item. If you have an emergency or need help, there will be guides throughout the area, so go to a safe point. These safe points are trees marked with yellow ribbons. On your mark, get set, go!"

The other guests took off in different directions as Wesley and Chanel stood glaring at each other.

She smacked her lips like a child. "I want another partner."

"Tough." Wesley straightened his backpack on his shoulders. "You're stuck with

me."

"Why do you have so much junk?" Chanel grabbed her satchel. "We're not going to the army."

"You should know I'm a man who likes to be prepared. You never know what might happen on these things. Come on." He rushed ahead of her. "We need to find the bank, so try to keep up. I hate to lose!"

He grinned as she grumbled behind him.

CHAPTER FIVE

"Come on, Slowpoke." Wesley stopped yet again to wait for Chanel to keep up. "It's not that difficult."

"Maybe not to you." She huffed and puffed, her sexy legs wobbling on the uneven trail. "God, it's hot." She fanned with her baseball cap. "Man, I thought this was supposed to be fun. I didn't know we'd be going uphill and shit."

Wesley snickered.

"Oh." She finally caught up to him and he purposely started off again so she couldn't catch her breath. "Come on, we need to rest!" She trekked behind him. "We've been out here for what... an hour?"

Wesley checked his watch. "Try fifteen minutes."

"No, that can't be right." She panted. "Oh, man. My side's hurting."

"You look like you'd be in better shape." Wesley hopped up the trail with ease.

"You're only thirty. I'm forty-two and I'm running rings around you."

"That's because... you got them long ass men's legs."

"You need to work on your conditioning, Sweetheart. Do some cardio."

"I exercise and don't call me 'sweetheart.' When you call me that, I hate it."

"I mean no harm."

"It's condescending." She struggled to walk uphill, and he finally helped her. "You don't call your male employees that, do you?"

"Fine." He let her go and continued on his mission. "Can't do anything right with you, can I?"

"You're just so oblivious." She huffed. "It's all about you. You don't even take time to think about anyone else."

He slowed down. "Here we go."

"It's true." She walked alongside him. "You know nothing about your employees. Not even those who've worked for Babcock since your father was alive. You damn sure don't know about *me*. Didn't even know I had a daughter, I bet."

"I knew." He stepped over a rock. "I just didn't know she was disabled."

"You didn't care."

"How can I care if I didn't know?" He cleared his throat. "What's her name?"

"Aria."

"That's a beautiful name."

"She's a beautiful young lady."

He smiled. "I bet she's strong and feisty too like her mother."

She caught his smile, but it seemed to make her madder. "Don't be all nice after the shit you said yesterday."

"I'm sorry about that. I was wrong. That was an awful thing to say."

She stumbled.

"I hated myself for saying it."

"You should. I didn't even know you could be that low."

He helped her after she tripped again. "If there's anything I can do, let me know."

She pushed him off. "Aria doesn't need your pity and don't act like you give a damn."

They stopped.

"You wouldn't even let me leave an hour early to take her to the hospital."

He took his backpack off. "What are you talking about?"

"Remember a month back when I said I needed to leave early? That it was an emergency? You yelled at me and told me if I left, I'd be fired." She stuck her chin in

the air. "Well, you know what? I left anyway, and Marcy covered for me. I don't care

who you are, but no one is going to stop me from helping my daughter."

"What was wrong with her?"

"She fell out of her chair at school and she has a spinal injury, so when she falls, she needs to be looked at immediately to make sure she's okay."

Wesley glanced around, scratching his wrist. "May I ask why she's in a wheelchair?"

"She has paraplegia. She's paralyzed from the waist down."

He sat on a rock. "What happened?"

Chanel squinted, the skin underneath her eyes vibrating. "Labor was terrible. She just wouldn't come out. I refused a C-section, so the doctor pulled her out with the forceps." She looked away, eyes watering. "And he damaged her spine."

"Ooh. God, I'm so sorry. So it was like a freak accident?"

"There's not a day that goes by that I don't regret the decision I made." She sat beside him. "If it hadn't been for me, she'd be walking and running like all the other kids. She's had many health issues, surgery, medications and pain." She lifted her head as a tear fell. "But thank God she's strong. She's stronger than I could ever be."

"She's strong like her mother." He rubbed his elbow against her. "And you cannot blame yourself for what happened. It just... happened. Things happen for a reason."

She wiped her eyes. "I tell myself that all the time, but mostly to make myself feel better."

He touched her knee. "I am very sorry for what I said about your daughter not belonging here."

"Yeah, that was low, Wesley."

"You know me. When I'm ticked off, I lash out without thinking. I didn't mean

it. Forgive me?"

"Yeah, but you do it again and my foot's gonna be up your ass."

He laughed. "I won't."

She grinned, revealing those sparkling teeth. "This dynamic between us is

weird. One minute we're fighting and the next we're talking like old friends."

"Sh." He winked. "I won't tell if you don't."

She laughed.

"Come on." He stood and grabbed his backpack. "I'll be damned if someone finds that piggy bank before we do."

"Oh, wait." Chanel pulled out her phone. "This is Aria."

She showed him a pic of a stunning young lady who had Chanel's glorious skin tone and smile.

"She's beautiful." Wesley looked at Chanel. "Just like her mother."

Chanel smiled but then, as if she reminded they weren't supposed to get along, she broke her gaze, got her bag and hurried ahead of him.

****

Aria carefully steered her chair through the rocky trail and came to the smooth walkway where she glided along at a comfortable speed. She heard laughter and chatter throughout the woods, but couldn't see anyone. As she rode, the voices got louder, and she smelled the musty, grassy odor of the lake.

"Aria!" Alex popped out from behind a pile of rocks and ran toward her. "Hey."

"Oh, hey."

He stood wide-legged in front of her chair with those big hiking boots planted into the earth. "What are you doing out here?"

"Nothing." She gripped her wheels. "Just rolling."

He grinned. "You out here alone?"

"Yeah. Why wouldn't I be?"

"Oh, I didn't mean nothing by it." The sun shined upon his silver stud earring, his rosy-brown hair cut into that spikey style all the Hollywood heartthrobs were wearing. "It's just that even I don't enjoy coming out here alone. It's kinda treacherous in some spots."

"Really?" Aria started off again. "Why are you out here alone, then?"

He pointed toward the lake. "Friends wanted me to meet them there."

"I see."

"Uh." He hopped in front of her, walking backwards as she crept forward. "Did you have fun playing volleyball yesterday?"

"Uh-huh." She snickered. "Why are you always blushing when I'm around?"

He straightened his composure and dropped his smile. "I'm not." He focused on her wheelchair with that awkward gaze.

"I have a spinal injury." She slowed her chair so she wouldn't run into him. "That's why I can't walk. I was born like this."

"Huh?"

"You wanted to know why I was in a wheelchair."

"No, uh—"

"It's okay. People always try to guess what happened to me. They wonder if I was in an accident or if someone shot me or something. I'm like this because the doctor got too crazy with the forceps, jerked me from my momma, and wrecked my spine. So I'm paralyzed from the waist down."

"God, that's terrible." He continued to back-walk in front of her. "Did your

parents sue him or anything?"

She shook her head. "And it's just my mother."

"Why didn't she take him to court? She'd have definitely won. You feel bad you can't walk?"

"Nope. How can you feel bad about something you never did?"

"True." He moved back beside her. "I bet people ask you that dumb question all the time."

"Not being able to walk means nothing. I can still do whatever I want."

"You're definitely not lacking in confidence, are you?"

She laughed. "You like my style?"

"What's not to like?" He pushed his hands into his pockets. "You're beautiful, witty and keep a guy guessing. Your boyfriend's lucky to have you."

"Nice try."

He chuckled. "What?"

"Trying to see if I have a boyfriend on the sly. If you wanna know, just ask."

"Okay, I'm asking. Do you have a boyfriend?"

She shook her head. "Not anymore. He cheated."

He grimaced.

"We can stop here for a bit." She stopped where she could enjoy the view of the

lake. "I see your friends down there acting silly."

"Yeah, that's all the time." He sat in the grass. "Aren't you gonna ask me if I have a girlfriend?"

"I don't care."

His face dropped.

"I didn't mean it like that." She smiled. "I meant that it doesn't matter. And I'm
sure a guy as hot as you has many girlfriends."

He half-grinned. "You think I'm hot?"

"Boy, please. You know you could put a model to shame. Don't tell me you haven't realized that in all these years."

He laughed, tearing off a blade of grass. "Well, I'm glad you don't have a guy."

"Why?"

"Just because." He looked up at her through his lashes. "I like you, Aria. You're a cool person."

"You don't know me, Alex."

"I'm getting to know you. That's why I wanna be honest. Do you know who I am?"

She snickered. "You're Alex."

"I mean, who my family is?"

She shook her head. "Someone rich, I'm sure."

"I'm a Stepford." He winced as if he expected her to yell at him. "You know? *The* Stepfords?"

Aria almost threw up a lung. "You mean of the billionaire Stepford family? Stepford Cosmetics? The world-wide multi-billion dollar empire? *Those* Stepfords?"

"I didn't wanna bring it up yesterday. I like the vibe we got, and I thought it might change if you knew the truth."

Aria gaped with her mouth open. "You're a Stepford?"

"See?" He stood, grass falling off his pants. "That's what I'm talking about. I'm not *just* a Stepford, Aria."

"This is weird. You're rich and you didn't want me to know? Alex, your family being successful is nothing to be ashamed of."

"I'm not ashamed of it. I wanted you to see *me*. I didn't want you liking me because of my family but because of who I am. I get that enough with the girls in my circle."

"Like Farrah?"

"Farrah's cool but it's these other high-society chicks. They're raised to catch a rich guy, so that's all they worry about. But they don't see the person I am inside. Even Dirk and Miguel take advantage of my status."

"Aren't they rich too?"

"Not as rich as me."

"Alex, Elon Musk isn't as rich as you."

"I mean, I'm not dumb. I know they hang out with me for the perks. But I get something out of it too because at least with them I can be myself. But with anyone else, I gotta put on this image because I represent my family. Well, I'm sick of representing my family. I'm my own person."

"Yes, you are." She touched his hand. "Trust me, you being filthy rich doesn't offend me in the slightest."

He laughed. "I know *you* wouldn't care. I just didn't want you to find out from someone else and be all weird."

"So you're the grandson, huh?" She whistled. "One day, that enormous fortune will be yours."

He shrugged and they continued their walk.

"My mother works for Babcock Electronics."

"Cool." Alex nodded. "My family's done tons of business with the Babcocks. Wesley's just as ruthless as his father was." He scratched his head. "What about *your* father?"

"What about him? I don't know where he is and never met him. Momma had me at fourteen and he ran off before I was born."

"It's his loss. So you can go hiking and stuff in your chair?"

"It's a hiking wheelchair." She sped up, and her wheel got caught on a rock and she almost tipped over. "Whoa!"

"Hey!" Alex grabbed her before she fell. "I got you. Are you okay?"

"Yes." She stared into his warm eyes. "This was worth the stumble."

"You ain't fooling me, Miss Adeyami." He stood straight. "You did that on purpose, so I'd grab you, didn't you?"

She hid her smile. "I plead the Fifth."

CHAPTER SIX

"Ah, shit." Chanel struggled through the walkway of jagged rocks and cracks. She'd fallen about 10 times already and wasn't in the mood to fall again. "Ouch." She stumbled. "Ooh, I hate this place!"

Wesley turned around, once again way ahead of her. "You okay?" He rushed to her. "You okay?"

"No." She pushed him away. "I don't think that damn thing is even out here. Probably a setup so they can have a bunch of grown people wandering around the woods looking stupid."

"No one's found the piggy bank yet." He checked his phone. "Jenna's supposed to send a text if someone finds it so we know to return."

"Hold on. I need a break." Chanel set her pack on the ground and got out another bottle of water and some crackers. "God, I'm beat." She sat on the grass. "You're not tired?"

"Let me see this." He snatched the crackers. "Peanut butter crackers?"

"Yeah." She took the sack back. "What's wrong with that? Peanut butter is full of protein, so it's healthy."

"*Natural* peanut butter is healthy." He dug into his bag. "Not that processed stuff full of oil, sugar, and sodium. You've been chomping on those all day. No wonder you can't keep up. Here." He handed her a half-empty bag of trail mix. "Trail mix with only natural sugars from the fruit. It'll keep your energy up without all the preservatives and crap."

"You're really into this fitness thing, aren't you?"

He sipped water, sweat trickling down his cheek. "Your body is your temple, and yours is too beautiful to waste."

She gaped in mid-chew. "Excuse me?"

He fidgeted as if he'd just realized what he said. "Huh?"

"Did you say my body was beautiful?"

"Uh." He stood erect, squinting. "No."

"Yes, you did. Ewe, gross. You've been checking me out, haven't you?"

"No, I'm your boss." He rolled his eyes. "It would be unethical."

"Oh, please, and you're not my boss anymore, remember?"

"I was wrong for firing you." He sat beside her. "You can have your job back."

"Nope." She tossed her chin in the air. "As long as that ramp is not in the front of the resort, I'm not interested."

"I told my people to schedule renovations to put a ramp in the front." He wiped the back of his neck with a rag. "Happy?"

"Why did you do that?"

"Because it was right. Jesus, can't anyone do something nice for you?"

"Wesley Babcock never does something without expecting something in return."

"Really?" He dabbed his forehead. "That's what you think of me?"

"That's who you are. You're the Wesley Babcock who lets nothing stand in his way. The guy that would sell his firstborn to score a deal. All you care about is your company, remember?"

"Hm. I see you don't know me as well as I thought."

"No, I know you very well, Mr. Babcock."

"You don't know shit. That's the problem with you, Chanel. You're too busy trying to tell people who they are instead of getting to know them."

"Oh, really? And it's pretty hard to get to know a man who seems to wake up in

the mornings just to be a pain in my ass!"

"You know what?" He stomped his foot. "You're a very nasty woman. Here I am trying to be nice to you and you're being the bitch you always are!"

"Bitch? Ooh!" She jumped up. "Your momma's a bitch."

"What did you say?" He stood, growling. "I dare you to say it again."

She got in his face. "I said your momma's a bitch. No wonder you're such an

asshole. You prove that all the money in the world can't fix a lack of home training!"

"That's it!" He threw his jug on the ground. "I don't take that shit from the wealthiest business leaders in the world, so I won't take it from you either! I tried to be nice. When I asked about your daughter, I was sincere."

"Bullshit, you said that to make yourself feel better. You do nothing for anyone but yourself!"

"Oh, and you're the picture of *unselfishness*? Don't make me laugh!"

"I do more for your ass than anyone else takes the time to do!"

"Oh, yeah?" he yelled in her face. "How do you figure *that*?"

"I put my whole life on hold for you, Bozo." She poked his chest with her finger. "Whenever you call, I'm there. No matter what I'm doing or what time of day. Even when you don't pay me for the extra time, I'm there!"

"I always pay you—"

"And you would be shit without me. You don't know jack about the money in your own company. If it wasn't for me and Louis, you wouldn't even know how much the company's worth!"

"That's it." He raised his arms. "That is it. I'm firing you again and I don't wanna see you until you pick your shit up from the job Tuesday morning. You hear me?" He snatched his bag and walked ahead.

"You can't leave me here!" Chanel jumped in place. "Wesley, come back here! We're a team. We gotta find the piggy bank!"

He marched on. "Kiss my ass, Miss Adeyami!"

"Oh, no!" she yelled, "You kiss *my* ass! Kiss it until your lips fall off you piece of crap!"

Wesley disappeared into the forest.

"Damn that man." Chanel sighed, looking around. "Where the hell am I?"

****

"You got fired *twice*?" Aria got chocolate ice cream from the fridge. "Mom, only you could get fired twice on your vacation."

"I don't wanna hear it." Chanel sat on the couch in the adjacent living room, rubbing her temples. "I got the worst headache I've ever had. Ooh, that man. I swear Wesley Babcock will be the death of me."

Aria snickered as she came from the kitchen.

"What are you laughing at?"

She dug her spoon into the half-gallon carton. "You like Mr. Babcock."

Chanel did a double-take. "W... what did you say?"

"You heard me." Aria licked her spoon. "You like Wesley Babcock. Might even be in love with him."

"Wait, a minute." Chanel chuckled, moving her hands around. "Did some alien come from out of space and steal your brain because you obviously no longer have one if you think I'm in love with Wesley Babcock."

"You don't find him attractive? You'd be the only woman that didn't."

"Why don't you just wheel your little ass in my room and get my aspirin? And stay out grown folks' business."

Aria sucked ice cream from the spoon. "You always get defensive when I'm right."

"Okay, enlighten me. What makes you think I want Wesley?"

Aria wiggled her eyebrows. "Got all the signs of a woman in love. You talk about Wesley constantly. Then, you jump every time he calls. You have a right to say no."

"I value my job. Has nothing to do with Wesley."

"And I hear you on the phone with Aunt Di." Aria slurped. "You told her you were having feelings for Wesley that you didn't understand. And it scared you."

"Is this what you do? Sneak around and listen to people's conversations?"

"It's true though. You feel something and maybe you don't wanna feel it, but you do."

Chanel sighed, looking away.

"Mom, I want you to be with someone who makes you happy. You need a life outside of just worrying about me."

"You don't even like Wesley."

"I'll put up with him if he makes you happy."

"Okay, stop, stop, stop." Chanel waved her hands. "You are wrong. I could never be with Wesley Babcock. We're not even from the same planet. Plus, he is so insensitive and selfish. He doesn't care about anyone but himself, and he left me in the woods today. So to hell with Wesley Babcock and I don't wanna talk about this anymore."

"Okay." Aria sat back in her chair, wiggling.

"You forgot to tell me where you were all day," Chanel said. "I called several times, and you didn't answer. Were you with that boy again?"

"What boy?"

"The one that kept you out for hours yesterday? What's his name?"

"He's nobody."

"Oh." Chanel scoffed. "So you can lecture me about Wesley but can't tell me about this boy. Do you like him?"

"Momma, I don't even know him."

"You know him enough to spend hours with him for two days straight. He's seen you more than I have. Who is he?"

She closed her eyes. "Alex Stepford."

"Stepford? As in the multibillion dollar cosmetics company? Those Stepfords?"

Aria nodded.

"Wow." Chanel touched her chest. "Man, the Stepfords are richer than Wesley."

"I don't even care about Alex's money. He's so down-to-earth and easy to talk to."

Chanel lifted her chin. "So you *do* like him?"

"I guess, but it's nothing." Aria laid the ice cream on the table. "I just like talking to him and it's so refreshing to be around a guy who sees *me* and not just my wheelchair."

"I wanna meet him."

"Why? Mom, he's just some guy I talk to at a resort. He's not my boyfriend or anything."

"I'm just floored at how much money these folks have." Chanel whistled. "I

mean look at the generational wealth we're talking about. What's the boy's name

again?"

"Alex."

"And he's the..."

"Grandson."

"Okay, he's the grandson." Chanel straightened up. "Which means he'll own the entire fortune one day. Wow. Look at that, Aria. They are so rich that their family will be rich for a hundred years or more. See, Alex will have children and then *they'll* be rich. Then *their* children will be rich and *their* children will be rich and goodness." Chanel shook her head. "You gotta give it to rich people. They know how to hang on to their money. They keep it in the family come hell or high water."

"He says all the right things, and he seems so nice, so I hope he's sincere. It's not like you'd let me date him, anyway."

"I didn't say you couldn't date, but I don't want you sneaking guys into the house."

"So I can date Alex?" Aria jerked forward, blushing. "I mean, if I wanted to?"

"I'd need to meet him first. A Stepford." Chanel gasped. "Never in my wildest dreams did I think we'd be close to the Babcocks and Stepfords."

"Alex invited me to the lounge later. His friends will be there."

"I was hoping we'd do some activities together. Isn't that the point of this trip?"

"We will." Aria went to the kitchen. "We'll do stuff tomorrow together."

"Okay, you can go, but don't get caught up." Chanel waved her finger. "You don't know this guy. And these rich dudes... you never know what they're up to."

"Alex isn't like that." Aria put the ice cream in the freezer. "I keep telling you, I'm a good judge of character."

"Yet you didn't know Richard was using you? Alex could do the same thing."

Aria got a cup of water. "What would Alex be using me for?"

"He could think you're easy or something. Rich people only have something to
do with people like us when they want something."

"It's not fair to judge Alex based on his finances." Aria entered the living room again. "And not fair to judge Wesley, either."

"What do you mean by that?"

"Just saying if we expect people to look beyond the surface with *us*, we need to do it with others, too."

CHAPTER SEVEN

Chanel refused to stay in the cabin all night. She'd paid to spend a weekend at The Village and she was going to make the most of it. She went to the recreational area, a long hallway on the side of the main building where you could receive dancing lessons, see a movie, play games, and just have fun.

Chanel loved games. Especially guessing games, so when she saw the sign that said "Truth and Lies Tonight", she hurried into the room.

Next to Truth or Dare, Truth and Lies was one of Chanel's favorite games. You partnered up, you said three statements about yourself, and your partner has to guess which one is true. She'd played it a few times on dates to break the ice and it was a humorous way to learn more about someone.

She smiled at the group of about 20 people who sat at the spaced out tables. Rhonda, the administrator, stood in front of the room, greeting people with a

big smile.

Chanel took a seat at the middle table and lo and behold, Wesley walked in.

Chanel groaned. "Seriously?"

Wesley rolled his eyes at Chanel and headed for the back table.

An enthusiastic Rhonda welcomed everyone and, of course, kissed up to Wesley along the way.

Chanel snuck glances over her shoulder at him and he glared back. She scoffed and turned back around.

"Now we're gonna have some fun tonight." Rhonda rubbed her hands together. "Whether or not you know the person you're paired with, you're bound to learn something about your partner." She walked through the tables, beaming. "You ready to play Truth and Lies?"

"Yes," the people yelled like school children.

"Great." Rhonda dashed back to the front table. "This is how it will go. I'll call up two people and you'll each say three things about yourself, but only one will be true. If your partner guesses which one is the truth, the team gets a point. Whichever team gets the most points wins half off for their next trip to The Village."

"Wow," Chanel said. "Pretty good."

"So let's get started." Rhonda picked three different pairs, and each one had hilarious results. It was cool to see how couples knew less about each other than the strangers in the room. "We're having fun, aren't we?" Rhonda laughed, scanning the room for more victims. "Okay, team number four will be... you." She pointed to Chanel. "What's your name?"

She stood. "Chanel."

"Chanel! Come on up."

Chanel hurried to the front, praying Wesley wouldn't be called next.

"Okay, let's make this interesting." Rhonda beckoned to Wesley. "Mr. Babcock! Why don't you join Chanel?"

Chanel dropped her head, hoping he'd refuse. Of course, he didn't. Why he seemed so eager to play this game was beyond her.

Then she realized... he wanted to embarrass her.

"Chanel, are you ready?" Rhonda giggled. "You go first."

Chanel sighed, avoiding Wesley's condescending stare. "Um, I love cotton candy. I went to Disney World when I was six. I once ate an entire large pizza in one sitting."

Wesley chuckled. "You went to Disney World when you were six."

Chanel jerked upright. "That's right."

Wesley lit up.

"Mr. Babcock?" Rhonda said. "Your turn."

He wiggled his shoulders. "I've never been to Paris. I love frog legs. I'm lactose intolerant."

The group laughed.

Chanel answered, "Either you've never been to Paris, which I find it hard to believe, or you love frog legs because you're not lactose intolerant. I've gotten you lunch plenty of times and you've never had an issue with dairy."

Wesley raised his eyebrow as if impressed she noticed that.

"You love frog legs?" She shrugged. "I guess."

He smiled, shaking his head.

"You've never been to *Paris*?" Chanel squealed. "You're kidding me."

"Nope. Been to France but not Paris."

"Okay, my turn." Chanel grinned, bouncing her feet. "I'm afraid of heights. I've been to Nigeria. I can't cook."

"I know you can *cook*." He smirked. "You cooked that Nigerian stew for the company Christmas party last year and it was amazing. Um, I'm guessing you've been to Nigeria to see your family, so you're afraid of heights?"

She shook her head. "I've never been to Nigeria."

"Really? Wow. Why haven't you gone?"

"Well, I haven't been in the financial space to go. Gotta save up money to take a big trip like that and when you're a single mother, it's difficult to save."

His brows pulled together. "You should see your family, Chanel. You and Aria should see where your family come from."

She rubbed her elbow, subconsciously. "Hopefully, I can one day. But seeing
how I no longer have a job, it won't be soon."

He sighed.

"Uh..." Rhonda smiled. "Let's continue. Mr. Babcock?"

He cleared his throat. "I'm scared of the dentist. The eighties were my favorite decade. I'm in love with someone."

Chanel flinched at how his tone changed with the last statement. "You're, uh... scared of the dentist."

"Nope."

"You loved the eighties?"

He shook his head. "I'm in love with someone. Rhonda, can we switch things up a bit? Make the game more exciting?"

She beamed. "Sure."

"How about we ask each other questions about ourselves?" Wesley said. "Chanel, are *you* in love with someone?"

"Excuse me?" Her voice cracked.

"You heard me." He fixed his gaze on her. "Are you in love with someone?"

"If I am, it's none of *your* business."

"This woman I want... you think I got a chance with her?"

She took in a shaky breath. "Rhonda, I don't wanna play this game."

"I don't either," Wesley said. "I'm tired of playing games, Chanel. Tired of

being around you and pretending."

Rhonda gaped.

Chanel whispered to Wesley, "What are you talking about?"

"We've been playing games with each other for months. Let's get to the truth.

Are you in love with me?"

The people gasped.

"*What?*" Chanel glanced at the group. "What the hell are you talking about?"

Wesley leaned forward, slumping those broad shoulders. "Do you think about me the same way I think about you?"

"Wesley." She trembled, her stomach in knots. "Stop this."

"No, I want you, Chanel. I care about you. You fight me at every turn. You challenge me, and that turns me on more than anything."

"This is crazy." She jumped out of the seat, and he grabbed her wrist before she could leave. "Let go of me, Wesley."

He stood. "Don't deny it, Chanel."

Everyone watched them with their mouths wide open.

"You want me too. I can feel it."

"Wesley!" She tried to break free but couldn't. "Let me go!"

"Denying it won't change things. Be honest with yourself. Tell the truth. You feel something for me. You want me too."

"Get off!" She snatched herself free. "You're crazy, Wesley. I don't know

what you're up to, but this isn't real."

"Chanel, you and me are the realist thing in my life right now." He moved closer to her. "I'm good at reading people, especially women, so you can't lie to me. You want me just as much as I want you." He touched her cheek. "And you're gonna come to me. You're gonna come to me because you can't fight this anymore than I can."

"Go to hell." She pushed him and looked at the shocked expressions staring from their tables. "How could you embarrass me like this?"

"I'm not trying to embarrass you, but I'm sick of hiding my feelings—"

"Stay away from me, Wesley." Chanel rushed out of the room. "Stay away!"

Of course, she knew Wesley wouldn't quit. Quitting wasn't in his nature. He wouldn't be so successful if it was.

With him running behind her, Chanel flew up the steps of cabin 12 and unlocked the door. "Go away, Wesley!" She leapt inside and tried to close the door but he grabbed it. "Stop!"

"No." He pulled on the door as she pushed it. "I won't let you run away from me anymore. We need to talk, Chanel." He shoved the door open, pushing her back. "Sweetheart, listen—"

"You won't leave?" She got out her cellphone. "I'm calling the police."

"Why? What are they gonna do?" He entered, kicking the door closed. "I own this damn place, remember?"

"Doesn't mean you have a right to bust in here like this." She ran behind the couch with the phone to her ear. "I don't wanna talk to you. You embarrassed the hell out of me!"

"Who cares about those people?"

"I care!" She shook the phone. "See, this is what I mean, Wesley. You never think about how your actions affect others. You tricked me."

"I didn't trick you." He walked to the coffee table. "Chanel, I've been holding my feelings in for months and I can't do it anymore. Why do we have to?"

"Maybe because I don't have feelings for you!" She marched from behind the couch. "You think of that?"

"One thing about you is you don't lie, Chanel." Sweat beads sprouted on top of his forehead. "So if you feel nothing for me then look me in the eye and say it."

She trembled, the phone shaking in her hand.

"Tell me you don't care about me, and I'll leave you alone."

She sucked in a breath and looked away.

"See?" His face brightened. "I know you're scared because it's been a while for you but it's been a while for me too. We can take this journey together."

"Are you insane? One moment you go from hating me to now you're in love with me?" She scoffed. "And I'm supposed to believe that though your actions haven't shown it?"

"I've shown it." He squinted. "When we were together, working alone all those times. You knew how I felt. You're too perceptive not to know."

She sighed.

"When we'd talk about stuff other than business, it felt like I've known you my whole life and I trust you, Chanel. I don't trust anyone else but Louis." He smirked. "I barely trust myself."

She hid her grin.

"I wanna be with you. My heart breaks when we're so close and I can't touch you."

She closed her eyes, her heart dancing to his charismatic words.

"You're a part of me, Chanel." He approached her and touched her face. "You are a part of me and I want us to be together."

"Wesley." Her words barely reached above a whisper. "We can't do this. It won't work."

"What are you afraid of?"

"I got too much shit to deal with. I got a daughter to take care of and a job to find—"

"Aria is not a baby and she can take care of herself if she's half as strong as

you." He caressed her face. "And your job will be there as long as you want it to be."

"Well, I don't want it." She pushed his hands away. "And I don't want you. You hear me, Wesley? I don't want this! I just want you to leave me alone."

"You don't mean that."

"Don't tell me what I mean." She moved away as he reached for her. "You're used to getting everything you want by snapping your fingers well I'm not some business for you to conquer. I'm a woman with my own mind and I don't need you. I don't need any man so please leave!" She pointed to the door. "Leave, Wesley!"

"Don't do this, Chanel—"

"Go!" She closed her eyes. "Now. I want you to leave, and then I'm gonna go down to the spa and have a massage and forget all about your ass. Now go. Go, Wesley!"

She expected him to object again, but he shuffled out the door without another word.

CHAPTER EIGHT

Aria entered the lounge, holding in her grin when she made eye contact with Alex, who drank a soda at the counter. He held his finger up, telling her to wait a minute, ordered her a drink, and walked over.

"Here you go, Madam." He handed her the cold drink. "Cherry soda."

"My favorite. You remembered."

He blushed, flexing his pecs through his black muscle shirt. "You look beautiful."

She looked down at her maroon peplum blouse and denim skirt. "Nothing spectacular."

"Anything looks good on you."

"Aria!" Farrah waved from the booth by the window. "Come join us!"

"Okay."

Alex blocked her. "Uh, I was hoping we could just hang out together."

"What's wrong? You don't want me with your friends?"

"Not really." He grimaced. "Farrah's okay, but Miguel and Dirk can be morons."

She chuckled. "It's fine. Besides, all teenage boys are jerks, so I'm used to it."

"Ooh." He gripped his chest. "Ouch."

Aria laughed as she rolled over to the booth. "Hi, everybody." She caught the snicker from Miguel, but played it off. "You guys doing okay?"

"Doing well." Dirk winked, putting his arm around Farrah's shoulders. "You looking pretty hot there, Aria."

"Thanks. What are you guys doing?"

"Just hanging out," Farrah said. "I'm glad you came. I get sick of hanging around these turds all day."

Alex rolled his eyes as he scooted into the booth.

"Alex says your mom works for Babcock," Dirk said. "Cool. Are you going to college?"

Aria nodded as she sipped. "Yeah, but I'm not leaving Sacramento. It'll probably be community college or something."

Miguel snickered again.

"What?" Alex asked. "What's so funny?"

"Nothing." Miguel straightened his shades on top of his big walnut head. "Community college is nice. What do you wanna do for your career?"

"I wanna be a counselor."

"Oh, that's nice," Farrah said. "Drug counselor, family—"

"I wanna counsel the inmates in prison."

Farrah gaped. "Really? What got you interested in that?"

"My uncle's in prison." Aria set her soda on the table. "Back in ninety-six, he was high on crack and he murdered a man and stole his car."

"Jesus," Alex whispered.

"I got some cousins in jail too, unfortunately," Aria said. "I'm all for people serving their time if they did something wrong, but the system is still behind with rehabilitation and access to in-prison counseling is essential."

"Counseling?" Miguel scoffed. "If you're out there killing and raping, I doubt counseling's gonna help. These monsters need to be thrown *under* the jail."

"Not everyone who commits a crime is a monster." Aria squinted. "People become victims of their environments."

"So you're saying they can't help themselves?" Dirk asked.

"No, but certain circumstances are hard to escape. Especially when you have to

deal with poverty, systematic racism, your neighborhood overrun by gangs and drugs, you don't have the choices everyone else does."

"That's bullshit," Miguel said. "We all have choices."

"Watch your mouth," Alex said.

"No, I don't buy that argument. If that's the case, how come some people who grow up in bad environments don't commit crimes and stuff?"

Aria glared at Miguel. "Because some people aren't as strong as others and you also gotta consider someone's upbringing." She looked at Alex, who smiled back at her. "The ones who don't go bad have stable home lives and decent role models. Or at least parents that can handle them and keep them out of the streets. Everyone isn't that fortune."

"I don't wanna hear that." Miguel sat back. "We all have the same choices and the same opportunities."

"You gotta be crazy to think that," Alex said. "You really think a person's environment and society doesn't affect how they end up? Systematic racism is real and society was designed to weaken the prosperity of minorities. You're Mexican and you don't see that? Or has all that money made you forget who you are?"

"To hell with you, Alex." Miguel grimaced. "I don't let my race define me."

"Nor do I," Aria said. "But I won't pretend this stuff doesn't exist."

"But you don't even come from the hood," Dirk said. "Alex says you live on Gaines Avenue. That's a pretty decent neighborhood. Why do you care about all this stuff if you've never experienced it?"

"You don't have to come from somewhere to care about it, Dumbass." Alex exhaled. "Aria, this is why I didn't wanna sit over here."

"What? We're not good enough for you now?" Dirk grinned while sipping his

drink. "Yeah, right."

"Shut up." Farrah nudged him with her elbow. "I think what you wanna do is wonderful, Aria. If we don't rehabilitate than the inmates will keep committing the

same crimes over and over. I commend you."

Aria smiled.

"I'm hungry." Miguel climbed out of the booth. "What you guys want? Pepperoni and sausage pizza?"

"Sounds good to me," Dirk said.

"Me too," Farrah said. "But only one slice for me." She patted her washboard stomach. "Gotta stay in shape."

"Mm, yeah." Dirk kissed her cheek. "I don't want my woman getting all fat."

"Shut up." She huffed, hitting his chest. "Aria, I love your blouse."

She beamed. "Thanks."

Alex leaned into Aria. "Is sausage and pepperoni what you want too?"

"Yes, that's fine." She smiled.

"Hey, Alex." Miguel gestured to him. "Come with me to make the order."

Alex winked at Aria as he stood. "I'll be right back."

She giggled as she watched him follow Miguel to the counter.

****

"Come here." Miguel beckoned for Alex to follow him around the corner and out of sight of the others. "Let me holler at you for a second."

"What is it?"

"What's going on here? Between you and wheels over there?"

"You're such a jerk. I like her. And?"

"No, I mean, what is this?" Miguel crossed his arms. "Are you falling for that

girl? Because that would be the dumbest thing you could do."

"Why do you say that?"

"Alex, come on. It's cool to *experiment* with her at The Village, but you know damn well you guys can't be together. Your parents would have a coronary if you brought her home. You don't fit."

"That's your opinion." He turned to leave and Miguel grabbed his shirt. "Get
off me!"

"I'm your friend, remember? It's my job to see things clearly, even when you don't. Break this shit off now. All you gonna do is hurt her because no way this will last."

"I like Aria, all right? She's amazing, and I can talk to her about anything. She understands me and doesn't give a shit who my family is or how much money I have."

"How do you know that?"

"Because she told me." Alex held his waist. "That's how I know. She's a genuine person. A hell of a lot better than those high-society bimbos my parents want me to date."

"*You* are a Stepford. It's not about *you*." Miguel poked him with his finger. "You got an image to uphold. You'll be the owner of Stepford Cosmetics one day. You can't be seen with just anybody and if you care about Aria, you'll quit her now before she gets hurt."

"Look, no one's talking marriage. But while we're here, I'm gonna enjoy my time with her."

"Oh, I see." Miguel grinned. "So this is about sex, huh? Wanna see if she is dead *between* the legs too, huh?"

Before Alex could blast Miguel for the crass remark, someone gasped from
behind him and he turned to see Aria staring straight at him with watery eyes. "Aria."

She whipped her chair in the opposite direction and sped out the door.

"Look what you did!" Alex pushed Miguel and ran after her. "Aria, wait!"

****

Aria raced through the walkway, struggling to see through her tears.

"Wait!" Alex ran up beside her and grabbed her wheelchair, forcing her to stop.

"Let me go!" Tears fell from her eyes. "I heard you, Alex!"

"What did you *hear*? If you're upset, you obviously didn't hear the whole

conversation."

"I heard enough! Is that what this is?" She looked up at him. "You just hanging with the girl in the wheelchair to see what I'd be like in bed?"

"No." He shook his head. "God no, Aria. Miguel said that shit. It was completely out of line. You know I really like you."

"Do I?"

"Yes!" He got on his knees in front of her. "Aria, I want you to be my girl."

She sniffled, touching the rhinestone pendant on her necklace. "I bet Miguel was saying I wasn't good enough for you, wasn't he? That I don't fit in your world and he's right. I don't."

"He's wrong." He lifted her chin. "Aria, I want you in my world. You've brightened it up. Before I met you, I was so depressed and lonely. Everyone else only sees me as a Stepford and not my own person. That means the world to me."

She shook her head as she wiped tears. "It's not realistic to think we can be together. We're just too different."

"We're alike where it matters." He caressed her hand. "I wanna give it a shot. I wanna be with you. Please, give me a chance."

"And what will your parents say when you show up with a black girl in a wheelchair? Something tells me they won't greet me with open arms."

"Our differences is why I like you. Aria, you are so strong and I admire you for your confidence and how positive you always are. You see your disability as strength, not weakness. I do too. But I don't see you as a girl in a wheelchair. I just see you as Aria. Isn't that what you've been searching for? For someone to see you for who you

really are?"

She looked into his eyes, sniffling.

"Where's that girl that came up to me asking for the ball? The one with all the confidence in the world that felt she can do anything and be anything? That's why I like you, Aria. Because despite all your obstacles, you keep going. You're braver than I ever could be. That's why... I love you." He put his arms around her and brought her closer to him.

She closed her eyes as the breath from his lips made her shiver. She welcomed the smell of his pinewood cologne as he nudged the tip of her lips with his as if to ask for permission. This wasn't her first kiss, but it was the first time emotion overtook her *before* the kiss happened. There had been so many questions, so many times of self-doubt, so many days of telling herself she wasn't good enough, but with Alex's kiss, she finally felt like she was. He could give her a thousand compliments, and they wouldn't have ignited her heart the way his touch did.

She heard the giggles of people who spied on them as they passed. Public displays of affection weren't Aria's style, but the kiss was so great and she cared about this boy so much that she didn't care.

Then she let doubt creep in again. She cursed herself for it, but it remained the old foe that never went away.

"I can't do this, Alex." She eased him away. "I was dreaming when I thought I belonged here with you, but I don't."

"You belong with me." He turned his head, readying to kiss her again. "I said I love you. I love you, Aria."

"In two days?"

"Yes." He kissed her again, and she broke away.

"I can't, Alex. Please move." She grabbed her wheels. "Please."

He pressed his lips together, staring at her as if he hoped his gaze would keep her from moving. "I love you."

Terrified at seeing the pain in his eyes, Aria continued on toward the cabins without looking back.

CHAPTER NINE

"This is why I should've kept my mouth shut." Wesley soaked in the hot tub behind his cabin that night while talking to Louis on speakerphone. "I poured my heart out to her and it was a complete disaster. Who the hell is she to reject me? *Me*?" He sipped from his slender glass of champagne. "I'm done."

"You can't be done," Louis said. "Not if you love her."

"To hell with love. People put so much damn emphasis on love, but all it does is cause pain." Wesley wiggled his legs in the soothing water. "For the first time, I thought I'd found someone who looked beyond my money to see *me*. And yes, it's been rocky between me and Chanel, but I thought she wanted me enough to take a chance, but I was wrong."

"So you're giving up? That's not the Wesley Babcock I know."

"I've accomplished stuff beyond most people's wildest dreams. I don't have to prove myself to Chanel Adeyami or any woman." He sunk deeper into the water. "I could give her anything she'd ever want or need. Working? She'd never have to work again unless she just wanted to. Aria's future would be set as well. I'd take care of her like she was my own daughter. I laid my heart out for Chanel to take and she turns her back on me."

"Gotta look at it from Chanel's point of view. You took her off guard."

"You were the one who said I needed to face my feelings."

"Yes, but telling her you loved her in front of a roomful of people was weird even for you, Wes. She's right, in a way. You don't think of how your actions affect other people."

"Fine." He sipped. "She won't have to worry about me embarrassing her again because I'm staying away from her. I'm sick of this rollercoaster ride with her. I'd love Chanel like no one ever has but to hell with her." He set down his glass and bobbed with the water up to his shoulders. "She wants to be alone and miserable for the rest of her life? So be it. I'm Wesley Babcock and I don't have to run after *any* woman."

****

Monday (The Last Day)

"Aria?" Chanel tapped on Aria's bedroom door that morning. Aria was usually up before Chanel so it wasn't normal for her to still be sleeping, so Chanel had the feeling something was wrong. "Honey?" She knocked again and when Aria didn't answer, Chanel inched the door open.

Aria sat in bed against the headboard, attention glued to her phone as always.

"I thought I told you I didn't want you on that phone with Joya all weekend talking about me," Chanel joked.

But Aria didn't crack a smile. "We're not talking about you." She texted like a maniac.

"You mind putting that up and talking to your momma?" Chanel sat beside her on the bed.

Aria exhaled and set her phone aside. "What is it?"

"You were already in bed when I got back from the spa last night." Chanel moved Aria's curly strands from her face. "You okay?"

"I was just tired."

"Aria." Chanel dipped her head, glaring at her. "You know you can't hide anything from me."

"You were right about Alex. I was fooling myself, thinking we'd be together."

"What did he do?"

"Nothing but his friends are jerks and it just reinforced how mismatched we

are. Alex is great, but we're just too different." Aria shrugged. "It's so confusing because he said he loved me."

"Loves you? Good Lord, you teenagers treat love like something you download off the Internet. That boy can't love you. He doesn't even know you."

"You can love someone without knowing them a million years, Mom."

"He's *infatuated* with you. Not in love."

"Momma, these feelings I have for Alex, I've never felt before. Everywhere I look, I see his face. Every time I close my eyes, I dream he's right here with me and his touch..." She closed her eyes. "My whole body feels like it's on fire and relaxed at the same time."

Chanel sighed, recognizing the feeling because it was the same way Wesley made *her* feel. "I did some digging and asked around about Alex."

"Mom." Aria scowled. "How could you do that?"

"I have every right to know about the boy my daughter is hanging around and I haven't met him *yet*. But, Alex seems like a good person."

"He's amazing." Aria's eyes brightened. "He's considerate, fun, sexy, anything you'd want in a guy." Her shoulders dropped.

"What?"

"Why torture myself thinking about him any longer? Once we leave, it's over. He says he wants me to be his girlfriend but..." She shook her head. "No."

"Aria, I want you to be happy." Chanel squeezed Aria's leg, wishing as always

she could've felt her comforting touch in that spot. "If it's meant for you and Alex to

be together, it'll happen."

"I heard what Mr. Babcock did." Aria raised her eyebrows. "He said he was in love with you in front of everyone?"

"I don't wanna talk about it."

"How do you feel about that?"

"I think it's insane, and he's up to something." Chanel drew her hand back. "I don't trust Wesley as far as I can throw him."

"That's not true. Mr. Babcock is a lot of things but he has a reputation of a loyal man who keeps his word no matter what. And I doubt he'd have a reason to confess his feelings in front of a crowd if he didn't mean it—"

"Just drop it, Aria. We came here to spend time together and we're farther apart now than when we came. So we're gonna spend the day together." Chanel poked Aria's side. "You and me."

"I thought you signed up for that nature hike today."

"I did, but you're more important." Chanel kissed Aria's forehead. "You need your momma. Hey, that spa is amazing. We should have a spa day. Wouldn't you like that?"

"I'm not in the mood."

"Don't let Alex get you down."

"I have a feeling if we go to the spa, I won't be much fun and I want you to have some fun, Momma. You go on your hike."

"No. You shouldn't be alone."

"Mom, we're at a resort full of people. I couldn't be alone if I tried."

"How am I going to enjoy a nature hike with you in here sulking?"

Aria combed her fingers through her frizzy hair. "Jeez, I gotta hurry and put on

my hair conditioner."

Chanel snickered. "You ain't lying. That hair's a mess. Were you sleeping or wrestling tigers all night long?"

Aria laughed.

"Oh, my baby." Chanel hugged her. "Cheer up, okay?"

"Go on the hike, Mom." Aria rubbed her mother's back. "You've been looking forward to this since we got here."

Chanel sat back. "You sure?"

Aria took Chanel's hand and smiled. "Have fun."

****

Chanel met with the small crowd in the woods that evening for the nature hike. The first thing she did was make sure Wesley wasn't there, and she was glad he wasn't. Sam, the enthusiastic guide, jumped around as if he weighed five pounds and with the energy of a kid who'd eaten a bag of sugar. It was obvious he loved his job and nature even more. He started off talking about his 13-year hiking expertise and traveling experience. Then shared stories of how he had to use unique survival tips to get out of different jams.

"Jesus," the woman beside Chanel whispered. "Looks like our guide could give Bear Grylls a run for his money."

Chanel grinned.

Finally, Sam stopped yakking and got to what Chanel had been waiting for, starting the hike. Sam read off the list of names to make sure everyone was present and then handed everyone maps and compasses.

"Seriously?" The young black guy with a flat top and diamond earring grumbled. "We're using maps and compasses? Why can't we use apps on our phones?"

"Because this is a true nature hike, not some video game." Sam smiled at Chanel as he handed her the items. "This is survival." He stalked back to the front of the group. "Our greatest explorers and journeymen didn't have apps." Sam stood wide-legged as he held his waist. "I know you millennials love your apps but live a little today, James, huh?"

James rolled his eyes.

"It's not just the millennials," the old rich geezer behind Chanel said. "I can't read a map to save my life."

The others nodded in agreement.

Sam gawked. "Are you kidding me? None of you can read maps?"

Chanel raised her hand. "I can."

Sam shook his head. "Okay, no big deal. If you wanna use an app, you can, but just stick close to me and you won't get lost or anything. Now remember, this is a nature hike. We'll be targeting some tough terrain, but nothing an amateur can't get through with my help. It will be challenging, though, for your mind and body." He rubbed his hands together. "Are you ready to be one with nature?"

Chanel looked around as the crowd groaned or shrugged.

Sam rolled his eyes. "Love that enthusiasm."

Chanel giggled.

"Remember all the rules I gave you and we're doing the buddy-system. Everyone stick with me or make sure you stick with someone else. Don't let this place fool you." Sam pointed to the forest behind him. "We might be by a resort, but this wilderness is real and you can get lost. There are also coyotes, rattlesnakes, and bears."

"*Bears?*" the platinum-blonde woman with the stiletto nails shrieked. "You didn't say nothing about bears."

Sam scoffed. "With those claws on your fingers, I doubt you'll have anything to worry about, Rosalie."

Everyone laughed.

"Contrary to popular belief," Sam announced. "Bears don't just walk up on you, but you need to be careful. Our path is safe, but if you stray, then you could run into trouble. I have everyone covered." He grabbed the sack behind him and gave everyone bear spray. "Please don't let fear take away your enjoyment. We'll be fine. Just listen to me. Do what I do. Okay?"

Wesley ran up with his backpack bouncing on his back. "I see I'm not too late. Sam, mind if I join you guys?"

Chanel exhaled. "I cannot believe this."

"Mr. Babcock!" Sam laughed, pulling Wesley forward. "Of course you can join us! If not for you, we wouldn't have this gorgeous place. Everyone, give Mr. Babcock a hand!"

Everyone clapped for him except Chanel.

"I hope I'm not interrupting." Wesley beamed at Chanel.

"No, we were just on our way. Let me get you your stuff." Sam handed Wesley the same items he'd given everyone else. "You got it everything, Mr. Babcock?"

He shook out his legs. "Oh, I'm ready."

Everyone laughed.

"Everyone ready?" Sam asked.

The grouped yelled back, "Yes!"

"Let's hit it, folks!" Sam turned around on his hiking boots and marched up the trail. "Be careful and watch your step. There are a lot of rocks in this area. You can twist your ankle before you know it."

Left behind with Wesley, Chanel rushed to catch up before losing sight of the group. She tried to beat Wesley, but that wasn't happening with those long-ass legs of his.

He grinned. "Are you seriously trying to outrun me?"

Chanel huffed, holding the straps of her backpack, which dug into her

shoulders. "What are you doing here?"

"I'm hiking." He strutted alongside her all nonchalant. "I told you I love nature. Ah." He took a deep breath. "Smell what God created. Isn't it breathtaking? Look at the view."

"Cut the crap, Wesley. You figured out I was here and showed up."

Sam's voice carried as he directed the group that were now way ahead of Chanel and Wesley.

"What is the point of this, Wesley?"

"Last night I was so angry that I never wanted to see you again." He rubbed his gloved hands together. "Then I remembered, you could be the love of my life. I can't let you go. We belong together, Chanel."

"Give me a break." She hurried to the group now standing by a small bush.

"See those?" Sam knelt down, pointing to prints in the dirt. "Those are coyote prints."

The group gaped in awe.

"So there are coyotes living right here in this space." Sam pointed down the trail. "There's a small lake around here so they walk through here for water."

"Where do coyotes live?" a woman asked.

"In dens." Sam stood straightening his pack. "They'll build them in tree trunks, rocks or occupy spaces already formed by other animals."

"Fascinating," Chanel said. When she turned and looked up at Wesley, he had that flirtatious smirk she wanted to smack off his face.

"Okay, let's keep moving." Sam trotted on. "Watch your step."

Chanel and Wesley fell to the back of the line.

"What do you want from me, Wesley?"

He rubbed up against Chanel as they walked. "A chance for me to show you I'm the man you need."

CHAPTER TEN

"I don't have time for distractions and I don't trust you," Chanel said.

Sam led the group across the road and into an even thicker forest.

"What do you want, Chanel?" Wesley asked. "In life? And don't say your job or anything to do with Aria."

The tip of her boot got caught in a crack and she stumbled.

"Whoa." Wesley helped her. "You okay?"

"Yeah." She moved away from him.

"Answer my question, Chanel. What do you want out of life? You have no identity outside of Aria and your job. I'm not criticizing because I'm the same way."

The group disappeared up ahead.

"It's pathetic," Wesley said. "I have all the money a person could want and run what *used* to be the most successful electronics company in the world, but I'm miserable."

She looked up at him.

"It's true what they say. Money can't buy love or make you forget about it." He huffed. "Wanna know why it's been so long since I've been with a woman? Because I'm afraid of intimacy."

Chanel squinted as the sun poked through the trees. "Intimacy?"

"Not sex, but of someone getting close to me. That's my deepest fear, so I push them away. Like I was trying to do with you, but my heart has other plans."

"Why are you afraid of intimacy?"

"I'm afraid that if folks get too close, they'll realize I'm not as fascinating as they think I am." He bumped into her as they squeezed through the California redwood trees. "That I'm just a normal person with a lot of baggage and low self-esteem."

Chanel popped some strawberry gum in her mouth. "No way in heck I'd believe *you* have low self-esteem."

"In business, I'm a tiger. I have all the confidence in the world. Nothing can stop me." He stuck out his chest. "But with love, I'm a pussycat scared to death."

"You're afraid of being vulnerable with someone." Chanel smiled, warmth coming over her because finally in a year she truly understood him. "It's because you have to be in control. You don't know how to function when you're not."

"You're the same way. That's why you want to run Aria's life. She's a young woman and you gotta cut the apron strings, Chanel."

"Says the man with no kids. What do you know about it?"

"You can hold someone so tightly that when you finally let go, they won't come around anymore."

She brushed off his opinion and continued toward the clearing. "There's a bridge ahead."

"Yep."

"Where is everyone?" Chanel looked around when they got to the rickety bridge, which hung over the rocky creek. "Shit, did we make a wrong turn somewhere?"

Wesley turned around, looking.

"Hello," Chanel yelled. "Sam? Hello! Sam!"

"I don't think he can hear you."

"Shit." She dropped her arms and looked at Wesley. "Where are we?"

He shrugged. "Looks like we're standing by a bridge."

She groaned. "I can see that. Stop playing. Where are we, and how do we get
out of here?"

He straightened his backpack. "How the hell should I know?"

"You own this place, don't you?"

"I own the resort and the surrounding property. I don't own all *this*. This is the wilderness, Chanel. I've never been out this far from the resort."

She pushed him. "You jerk. Stop playing around and get us out of here."

"I don't know where we are!"

Chanel got out the map but that was no help and she threw it back in her bag when she became frustrated.

"You can read maps?" Wesley asked. "I can't understand a map to save my life."

"You're cracking jokes when we're *lost*?" Chanel hopped around, yelling for the others. "Help!"

Wesley flinched, covering his ears. "Except for giving me a pounding headache, what is the purpose of your screeching?"

"We're lost in case you haven't noticed!"

"Just calm down." He grabbed her shoulders. "Take a deep breath. The resort isn't that far from here. It's not like we're miles away from civilization."

"It feels like it." Chanel turned around in circles. "We don't know how long we'll be out here."

"Chanel, calm down."

"No," she squealed. "This happens all the time where people went on hikes and ended up trapped for days. The weather got bad, or they got hurt. And they were close to some park or resort, too. It can happen, Wesley. It can happen!"

"Sh." He held her still. "Nothing bad is going to happen. The others are out here somewhere. I'm sure we'll run into them if we keep going. The good thing is it's not even the afternoon yet, so we got plenty of daylight. First step is..." He got his phone. "Ta-da! We have cellphones, remember? I'll call the resort and let them know we're lost and have them send out a search party."

"Okay." Chanel huffed and puffed. "Sounds good."

"Uh-oh." Wesley frowned at his phone. "Um—"

"Please don't tell me you don't have a signal."

"A signal? It's dead as a doorknob." He held it up. "I forgot to charge it."

"Dead?" Chanel shrieked. "How the hell can it be dead when you are on that thing every minute of the day? You don't go anywhere without checking that damn phone. It's the only thing you seem to care about and now the one time this is life or death, it's dead! What idiot comes out to the woods and doesn't check his damn phone?"

"Instead of yelling at me, you can check yours."

Chanel got hers out of the back pocket of her shorts. "No signal." She tapped it. "I don't know why this day and age they still make phones that can't keep a damn signal in the woods!"

"Just too many trees around here."

"Now, what are we gonna do?"

Wesley put his hands on his waist and shifted his weight to one side. "We gotta walk over the bridge."

"That thing looks like it's been hanging there for a hundred years. What if we fall?"

"I'm sure Sam and the group crossed the bridge."

"Let's just go back." Chanel turned back to the thicket.

"We're too far out to go back. I say we keep going and try to run into the

others. I bet they miss us, too."

"That's nuts." Chanel stomped her foot. "It's smarter to go back to where we came from. Why venture out further?"

"I'm telling you, we are too far from the resort to go back. You know your way back from here exactly? I sure as hell don't. You see all those trails we crossed? The group is out here, Chanel." He stomped *his* feet. "Let's just keep going until we find them."

"No." She pointed toward the forest. "I'm going back to where we came from."

"Whatever. I'm going on the bridge." Wesley stomped toward the bridge, walked across a few planks and as he put his foot on another, the plank came loose and Wesley's leg fell through the gap as he struggled to hold himself up. "Ah!"

"Wesley!" Chanel sprung onto the fence and crawled to him. "Wesley, are you all right?"

"Maybe you were right." He grunted as he struggled to hold on. "Crossing the bridge might not have been a good idea after all."

"Come here." Chanel gripped his wrists, but he was so big there was no way she'd be able to pull him up alone. "I'll hold you best I can, but you gotta get yourself up. Come on."

Wesley grunted, sweat falling from underneath his baseball cap as he struggled to pull himself up. "Ah, help me, Chanel."

"I'm... trying." She heaved. "You're about a foot bigger and a hundred pounds heavier than me."

Wesley strained, the veins popping out of his forehead. "I... I think I got it." Holding his breath, he pulled himself up to where he could bring his leg out of the hole. "Oh."

Chanel grabbed him. "You all right?"

"Yeah." He waited a second to settle his breathing, then leaned up on his hands. "Help me up if you can."

Chanel pulled on him as he attempted to stand, but stumbled back and

tumbled over with Wesley toppling on top of her. "Oh!"

Wesley stared at her with a blissful haze coming over his face.

He'd probably been stroking Chanel's ponytail for minutes before she realized it.

Everything stopped around them, nature falling silent. Wesley pressed his muscular frame on hers, and Chanel froze in time, their bodies so intertwined she could hear his heartbeat.

Wesley slightly turned his head to the side, bringing his lips closer for a kiss.

Chanel jerked her head in the opposite direction. "Come on, get up."

Wesley moved in closer. "Why?"

"I'm serious." She pulled at his shirt, but no way could she move if he didn't allow it. "We gotta find the others. We can't be laying on this bridge like this. The whole thing could collapse."

He outlined her chin with his thumb. "Wouldn't it be worth it?"

Chanel couldn't look him in the face now because she'd surely lose the battle. And right now, on this bridge wasn't the time or place. "Please, Wesley." She held her breath. "Get off me."

His right eye twitched, and he punched the planks beside her as if it were all he could do to hold in his anger as he moved off of her. He stood over her, looking down at her with more frustration than she'd ever seen from him. "Let's go." He put on his backpack.

"You're..." Chanel stood, fixing her clothes. "You're not mad, are you?"

"No."

She touched his arm. "Yes you are."

"I am not *mad*," he snapped. "Besides, we got more important things to think about than a kiss."

She anxiously rubbed her hands. "I'm just not ready for all this."

He glared at her. "Ready for what?"

"For whatever you want this to be."

"You mean love?" He scoffed. "Something tells me you'll never be ready for that."

He walked back in the direction that came from.

****

Aria sat on the deck, watching resort guests race each other in the water, when someone knocked on the cabin door. "Come in!"

A second later, Alex appeared on the deck. "Hey. What are you doing?"

"Nothing." She turned back around, watching the fun in the water. "Just enjoying one of my favorite Nigerian snacks." She held up the warm ball of fried dough.

"Looks like donut holes."

"They're Nigerian donuts, you could say. Puff-Puff."

"Puff-Puff?" He snickered, sitting in the lawn chair beside her. "Where you get them from?"

"I made them at home for the trip." She handed him one. "They're a guilty pleasure. Taste it."

Alex bit into it and chewed. "Mm. It's dense. Kinda like a cake donut."

Aria licked her fingers. "This is my comfort food. I eat them when I'm happy, sad, confused."

"I can see why. Can I have another one?"

She held the bowl out to him and he grabbed a fat one.

"So what's the reason you're eating these today?" He chewed. "Sad? You don't have to be because I'm not letting you go."

"Alex—"

"I've never felt for anyone like I do you, Aria."

She straightened up in her wheelchair, grinning. "We're only teenagers."

"I'd feel the same no matter how old we are. I wanna be with you. That's all I know. I'm not quitting. One thing I learned from my family is to always go after what I want, no matter what." He dipped his head. "Aria, we'll both be leaving The Village tomorrow. We can't leave like this."

"It's best if you forget me."

"Can a man forget his heart?"

She grinned as she chewed.

"Okay, that was corny." He laughed. "I'm not pressuring you to be my girlfriend right now. You can think about it. I just want us to stay in touch after we leave. As friends."

She held in her smile.

"What do you say?"

"What I've enjoyed about us is that we let the moment decide naturally. So let's keep doing that."

"Okay." He blushed. "They're having a ball out there, huh? I love swimming."

"Me too."

He jerked his head toward her. "You can swim?"

"Yeah."

He gave her the once-over. "But you're paralyzed."

"You don't need your legs to swim contrary to popular belief." She set the bowl of Puff-Puff on the table. "Are you challenging me?"

He batted his eyes. "What?"

Aria looked out into the lake. "Like you said, it is our last day, so why waste it?"

"You're serious? You wanna go swimming in the lake?"

"Don't you wanna see me in my bikini?"

He licked the corner of his mouth. "Is that a trick question?"

CHAPTER ELEVEN

Chanel followed Wesley up and down the forest. They had left no markings when they first came, so every tree and rock looked exactly the same. Wesley said little to her since the bridge and every time he looked at her, he seemed to get more frustrated. Yet, what did he expect? For her just to forget her qualms and make love to him? Once again, it was all about him. He was so used to getting what he wanted he couldn't fathom Chanel rejected him.

She meandered through trails, her toes cramping in her tight hiking boots.

What? Did he think it was easy for her to reject him? Hell no. Under any other circumstances, the outcome might be different. Because she'd be a fool to not treat herself to Wesley at least once. If just to test just how much he really loved her.

He looked back at her and asked how she was doing. Perhaps she'd been too quiet.

"I'm fine."

He faced forward. "This is ridiculous. The group's gotta be here somewhere."

"Wanna check our phones again?" Chanel stopped and checked hers. "No signal."

"No need to check mine if it's dead." He stopped by a bush of wild roses native to California. "We've been walking in circles for at least two hours. Let's take a break. I'm thirsty. What you got to eat?"

She took off her pack. "Just some nuts and a ham and cheese sandwich."

"I got some trail mix, granola bars, sardines—"

She grimaced. "Sardines?"

"We stay out here long enough and you'll eat them."

They got out the food and sat beside each other on another huge rock.

81

"Lost or not, this is gorgeous." Chanel bit into her sandwich made with tangy sandwich spread. "I can see why you'd buy a resort out here."

"Not to alarm you..." He chewed trail mix. "But we might have to stay the night."

"Shut up." She gaped. "You can't be serious."

He checked his watch. "Only a few more hours of daylight left, and it's gonna be too dangerous to be walking around at night."

"Dangerous?" She looked around, remembering the coyotes, snakes and bears. "This is just great. What a weekend. You show up, I get fired, and now I'm lost."

"What's your biggest wish?" He chomped. "Something you've always wanted?"

She looked up toward the sun. "To go to Nigeria and meet the rest of my family. I've met a few that visited the US but not the others." She kicked out her leg.

"We all can't hop on our private jet or helicopter any time we want."

"What if I gave you the money? Would you go?"

"No."

He winced as he chewed. "Why not?"

"Because I'd never take your money." She scratched her leg as something bit her. "I'm not a charity case, Wesley. I know you're used to your money being the answer to everything, but it's not with me."

"Jesus, Chanel, I was being nice, not trying to offend. I don't know why I even bother."

"I didn't say it wasn't nice to *offer*." She bit into her sandwich. "But I've been making my way all this time. I'm fine."

"Everyone needs help."

"Even you?"

He sighed, looking out into the distance.

"Wesley, what's wrong? I feel you've had something on your mind for a while. Even before we came here."

He wiped his hands on his pants. "Babcock Electronics probably won't be around in a few years."

"What?"

"Difficult to admit going from the biggest electronics company to losing more money than you bring in."

"I do the books, remember? I know Babcock's been losing money, but not enough to close. And a lot of businesses are in the same pickle. You've gotten out of pinches before. You'll do it again. The investors won't let anything happen to the company either."

"You don't get it." He shook his head. "You do the books but you haven't seen

everything. I was embarrassed to let you see how big of a failure things have become so I let Louis handle some of the accounting." He avoided eye contact. "So you wouldn't know."

"Wait, a minute. Are you saying you *hid* financial stuff from me? Your accountant? Wesley, that's so dishonest."

"I was embarrassed, Chanel. I care more about what you think than anyone

else, and I didn't want you to think I was a failure."

"So you hid something his big from me?" She wrapped up the rest of her sandwich after losing her appetite. "Wesley, you see how screwed up that is? You didn't take me seriously as your employee. I'm not some kid you gotta shield things from."

"It wasn't about you. It was about me." He wiggled his leg. "I was ashamed. I

could lose everything."

"That won't happen."

"Babcock Electronics did great for generations. Then under my leadership it fails?"

"It's not because of *you*." She touched his shoulder. "These things happen. It's not mismanagement or anything. The economy sucks right now."

"But it's sucked many times and Babcock has survived."

"It'll survive now too. Wesley, if you don't believe that, then there's nothing else I can say. I guess I believe in you more than you believe in yourself." She opened her Thermos and sipped. "The man I love wouldn't give up so easily—"

"What?" He jerked up straight. "What did you say?"

Chanel swallowed water.

Shit. Did that really just come out of my mouth?

"Uh, we should probably get going." Chanel hurriedly screwed the top back on her Thermos. "As you said, daylight won't be here forever."

"Uh-uh." He touched her knee. "I heard what you said. You said, 'The man I love wouldn't give up so easily.' That's not a slip-up, Chanel."

"It is too, I misspoke. I meant to say, 'The man I respected.'"

"Bull." He rubbed her knee. "I always knew you loved me, but now no matter how much you try to, you can't deny it."

"This isn't the time for this, Wesley." She cleaned up her littering. "We need to find the others. I don't wanna be stuck out here all night. Do you?"

He held a quizzical smile, eyes in a daze. "I wouldn't mind if we got stuck here a little while longer."

She sighed.

****

"Ah." Alex climbed out the lake, water dripping from his powerful shoulders and down his red swim trunks. "Here you go." He lifted Aria out of the water and laid her on the blanket on the shore. "You were right. You are an excellent swimmer."

"Thank you." She dried her face with her towel and flexed her arm muscles. "One benefit to being in a wheelchair is you build up your upper body, so I'm a strong swimmer with or without working legs."

"Well, I'm impressed." Alex lay beside her. The water had turned the spikes in his hair into damp bangs. "Then again, everything about you impresses me. I learn something from you every day."

Aria leaned back on her elbows, watching the guests playing in the water. "This

weekend has been the best I've had. I'd love to come back, but since Wesley fired my momma, I don't know."

"You can come back with *me*." He kissed her hand. "What's up with your mom and Babcock, anyway?"

"She's in love with him and afraid to admit it." Aria scratched her shoulder. "I could tell she liked him from the start."

"I rarely pay attention to what my parents talk about." Alex chuckled. "But the rich gossip too, you know?"

"Really?" Aria snickered. "I never would've guessed that."

"Babcock Electronics isn't doing so well. Might end up closing."

"What?"

"Yeah, he's bleeding money. Your mom didn't tell you?"

"She said things were slow, but I didn't know it was that serious. Wesley's obsessed with that company. He's never been married or had kids because he's put his whole life into it. Must be devastating to be so close to losing something you care so much about. He's a jerk, but I feel bad for him."

"Yeah, well, there's more to life than making money and having companies." Alex leaned back on his elbows. "Like this. Just being able to sit down and enjoy life. I never get to do this at home. Either I'm going to some event for my parents or I'm struggling to keep up that image everyone expects. That's why I admire you." He smiled. "You're just you and don't care what people think."

"I used to, but then I realized people will think what they want about

you regardless, so why not be yourself?" She shrugged. "We owe nothing to anyone."

"No we don't." He caressed her back.

Aria tingled, and she could guess what he was about to say.

"All I've been thinking about is that kiss," he said. "It was the best I ever had."

"Come on. All the girls you must've gone out with? Some, I'm sure, are way more experienced than I am." Her heart pounded as he moved his hand to the curve of her back. She didn't even care they were in public. "I'm a virgin," she blurted out.

He chuckled. "I'm not."

She fidgeted. "I just wanted to let you know."

He leaned into her. "Must be a reason you wanted me to know that."

"That guy who cheated on me, Richard, he was pressuring me into sex and I almost slept with him to please him."

Alex's forehead wrinkled.

"Then I remembered what my mother went through and how she always told me I didn't have to sleep with a guy for him to be with me."

"You don't." He pinched her chin. "Any man would be lucky to have you."

"I guess, I'm trying to say, that with you, it's different. My stomach ties up in knots when I look at you. My knees shake when I hear your voice. I get all these thoughts about living a life with you and when we're together, nothing else matters."

"Aria?" He laid his forehead on hers. "Do you wanna sleep with me?"

She shivered, sucking her lip.

"I want you." He pulled her close. "But I am not with you for sex. I'll wait. As long as it takes. I'll be here if I got to wait years until you're ready."

Her breathing quickened, and she felt as if her chest were closing in on her. "What if I *am* ready?"

He batted his eyes.

"I'm sixteen and I've never been in love until now." She clasped his hand. "I wanna be your girlfriend if you still want me to be."

"Course I do." He kissed her, sucking water from her lips. "I want that more than anything, but you don't have to sleep with me, Aria."

"I know but I just meant it could lead to that. I've never felt this way before, Alex."

"Me either."

"Let's go back to the cabin. Spend our last day together alone."

He smiled, inching in for a kiss.

"Aria!" Farrah ran up, kicking up dirt with her bare feet.

"Farrah, what's wrong?" Alex asked.

"I just came from the front desk." She panted. "Sam, who led the nature hike your mother went on, he says she and Mr. Babcock are missing."

"What?" Aria swerved her chair around in Farrah's direction. "What happened? Is she okay?"

"Apparently, she and Babcock got separated from the group hours ago."

"Hours?" Alex scowled.

"Alex," Aria shrieked. "My mother is missing! Oh, God."

"Hold on. Don't get upset." Alex patted her shoulder. "I mean, we're at a resort.

What could happen?"

"Alex! Some wild animal could eat her!"

"Aria." He bent down, looking her in the face. "Calm down. I'm sure she's fine."

"I gotta talk to Sam. Help me into my chair."

"Okay." Alex picked her up. "But I'm coming with you."

CHAPTER TWELVE

"Chanel!" Wesley called from behind her. "Honey, we're going in circles."

"This is impossible!" she yelled. "How the hell can we not get out of this place? Do you remember this tree?" She pointed to the sapling. "We didn't pass it before, did we?"

Wesley turned in a circle, pointing to other saplings that looked just like it. "You mean like this one, this one, and this one? Chanel, they all look alike. Every goddamn tree in this place looks alike!"

"Here's a tip, Wesley." She charged him. "If you're gonna buy a resort, you might wanna pick a location where people won't get lost in!"

"Well, *sweetie...*" He bared his teeth. "No one besides us has been stupid enough to get lost!"

"This is all your fault! If you hadn't barged into the hike, none of this would've happened!"

"How is it *my* fault?"

"Because I was paying attention to *you* and lost the group!" Chanel pointed into the distance. "So yes, yes, this is your fault, Wesley. I'm sick of you! Every time I turned around this weekend, there you were in my face. What is it going to take for me to get rid of you?"

"You're not exactly a treat to be around, either." He threw his backpack on the grass. "There are a lot of things I'd rather be doing than fighting with you!"

"Ooh!" Chanel jumped up and down. "I knew I shouldn't have ever taken that job! Ever since then, you've been a thorn in my ass. I'm so glad I'm fired!"

"Not as glad as I am, Honey Bunch! You being fired is the best gift I've ever given to myself!"

"Oh, yeah?"

"Yeah!"

They turned their backs to each other and crossed their arms. A minute later, Wesley started laughing and, though Chanel tried to fight it, she joined in.

"Look at us," she said. "Like two spoiled toddlers."

Wesley chuckled. "What can I say? You bring the best out of me."

They faced each other.

Chanel sighed. "It'll be dark soon. I'm scared, Wesley."

"Don't be scared. I won't let anything happen to you. Check this out." He dug into his pack and pulled out a silver Glock handgun.

"Wesley, what the hell?"

"I got us covered." He waved it around. "So you don't have to worry."

"Stop waving that thing before you shoot me with it! You got a gun?"

"You'll be glad I do if a bear or something shows up in the middle of the night."

Chanel groaned, hugging herself. "You mean we're gonna have to stay here all *night*?"

"Maybe." His eyebrows fell into straight lines. "We'll be okay. They'll find us in the morning."

"If we're not bear or coyote food by then."

He grinned, hugging her. "I'm not gonna let anything happen to you. You trust me?"

She nodded, taking advantage of his firm embrace. It had been so long since a man held her.

"Looks like our priorities have shifted from finding the group to finding a place

to camp." He shrugged. "We got tents, food, and I can make a fire. We'll be fine."

"What if no one ever finds us and we're stuck out here for years like Tom Hanks?"

He laughed. "This is California not a deserted island. Even if we can't find our way out, hikers come through here all the time."

"God. Aria. She's probably worried to death. I haven't been able to call her." Chanel checked her phone. "I still have no signal. I wonder how she's doing. If she's okay—"

"Aria's fine." Wesley put the gun in his back pocket. "We gotta find somewhere to camp and I don't like this spot." He looked down at the muddy grass. "Mud means there's water around here and if there is water, there are animals."

"Yep. You want to be close to a water source but not too close to where an animal comes up to your camp."

Wesley gaped. "I'm impressed. You have survival skills."

"Please." She held her waist. "I learned that from *Naked and Afraid.*"

"*Naked and Afraid*?" He laughed. "I love that show! Never missed an episode."

"Get out of here. You watch *Naked and Afraid*?"

"Seen every episode and all the spinoffs." He stuck out his chest. "*XL* is my favorite."

"Mine too." Chanel shrugged. "I even thought about auditioning."

"*Well.*" He looked her over. "You got the body for it."

"Cool it." She chuckled. "We're not gonna spend the entire night with you flirting, are we?"

He put his backpack on his shoulder. "I make no promises."

****

Right as the sun went down, Chanel and Wesley found a cozy clearing behind
some large boulders naturally stacked around it to form a wall.

Wesley easily made a fire with his cigarette lighter, reminding Chanel of how much he smoked, and then they settled into their sleeping bags while eating Wesley's granola bars and Chanel's peanut butter crackers for dinner.

The two sat close together, Chanel not realizing just how close until she got that tingle in her stomach again.

"I'm almost out of water." She shook her almost-empty Thermos.

Wesley shook his too. "We have to ration the little we have then. If push comes to shove, I can get some out the lake and purify it."

"Surely we won't be here *that* long." Chanel stretched out her legs. "I can't remember the last time I've been so tired."

Wesley ate a cracker. "This isn't so bad, right? If we gotta be stuck here for a night, this is the place to be."

"Ouch." Chanel smacked the side of her neck. "It's nice except for the bugs."

She broke the plain granola bar in half. "You still smoking?"

He rubbed the back of his neck. "Nah. Well, *trying* not to."

"Why are you stopping? Because I told you how unhealthy it was?"

"I only did it for my anxiety. It's difficult leading a company, and I get stressed out. Least I'm not a drunk, right?" He laid his head back on the rock. "I can't wait to meet Aria. I hope she likes me."

She laughed, covering her mouth.

"What? Don't tell me you've poisoned that child against me."

"*I* did nothing. She thinks you take advantage of me."

"So I'm gonna have to win her over, huh?"

Chanel looked up at him, his million-dollar smile glistening in the light of
the fire. "Why would you have to win her over?"

"You know why." He wiggled against the rock to get comfortable. "Can't be with you and have your daughter hating me, right?"

"So it's a given we're gonna be together?" She dusted crumbs off her hands. "Because you say so? Can't let go of that control, huh?"

"If I didn't force the issue, there would be no movement. Hell, I'm tired of waiting. I want us to be together." He took off his cap. "I put it out there so now the ball's in your court."

"Why?" She laid her head on the rock beside him. "Why do you wanna be with me? And don't say same lame crap you got from a Hallmark card. I want the truth."

"You're the strongest person I've ever met and that makes me want you more than anything."

She grinned to herself.

"You've gone through shit I couldn't even imagine. Raising a disabled daughter

all on your own. Then becoming a successful accountant. What drives you, Chanel? What's inside you that refuses to give up?"

"I was fourteen-years-old when I had Aria and her father was eighteen. I told him I was pregnant and a week later, he was gone."

Wesley flinched.

"Supposedly he went to the army, and I never heard from him again. Course, I had other things to deal with, like the way my father looked at me when I told him about the baby." She exhaled, eyes tingling from tears as she went back to the hardest moment of her life. "See, my dad has strong Nigerian pride." She stuck her shoulders in the air, mocking her dad. "Strong traditional values and he's very conservative. There's no gray with him, just black and white. Right and wrong. I'll never forget how he looked at me when I told him I was pregnant. That look... it wasn't disappointment. It was like he didn't *know* me anymore." A tear fell. "Like he was looking at a stranger and it cut right through me as if he'd sliced me open with a knife."

Wesley tucked in his lips.

"It hurt, Wesley." She sniffed. "It hurt more than anything."

"So, what did you do?"

"I did the opposite of what some girls would do. I decided then and there I wouldn't be a statistic. My dad had given up on me. He'd fought hard to make it in America. Had a Masters in Computer Science and Mathematics and was a successful professor at the community college."

Wesley smiled.

"He'd come from nothing in Nigeria to owning his own home, getting married, and having a daughter and not one day went by that he didn't remind me what he expected of me. And when I told him I was pregnant, it was like he gave up on me. But, oh no. No." She shook her head. "I was determined to prove him wrong. He expected me to fail because he saw all mistakes as failure."

Wesley grimaced.

"But no one was writing my story but me." She pointed to herself. "So the first

thing I did was finish high school. Yes. My mother didn't work, so she took care of Aria until I graduated. And I graduated with a four-point GPA."

"Dang." Wesley scratched behind his ear. "I can't even remember my GPA, but I know it sure as hell wasn't that high. Probably two-point." He laughed. "Guess it's a good thing I inherited a company, right?"

"My dad still looked at me with disgust, but that was fine. I got student loans,

and I packed by daughter up and went to Austin. I got my degree in accounting at

UT Austin graduating with honors."

Wesley clapped with a bright smile.

"I went to school during the day and I went to work at night and I supported Aria and myself *by* myself." She popped a cracker into her mouth.

"Wait, so you went to work, went to school and did all that studying and took care of a disabled child all on your own?"

"With just student loans and what I made cooking catfish at the seafood restaurant."

"Wow. I don't know if I could've done all that."

"After graduation, I came back to California, worked at a couple of accounting firms and then got the job with you."

Wesley stroked her cheek with his thumb. "Me hiring you was the best decision I made. What about your father?"

"Oh, he still has that look in his eyes sometimes. But I don't care anymore. I'd won." She smiled. "I proved him wrong and no matter what happens, he'll never doubt me again. I bet you that." She looked up again to see Wesley staring at her with an unleashed hunger in his eyes she'd never seen before. "What?"

She barely got the word out before his lips were on hers. She pushed at his chest. Yes, her first instinct was to push him away, but she stopped. Because she was tired of fighting him. Tired of running from how he made every hair on her body stand up whenever she *thought* of touching him.

His kisses were rough, wet, and sloppy. Not in control, like his style of dress or the way he commanded business.

He wrapped her in his arms, smothering her in his heat. All the while, his lips

stayed on hers as if he'd die if he let her go.

An agonizing moan sputtered from Chanel's lips as he lifted her top over her head and laid it beside him. Then he struggled with his T-shirt, pulling and stretching as if he couldn't get it off fast enough.

Moaning, Chanel grabbed his face and pulled those lips to hers again. Damn liar had snuck a smoke at some point. He smelled more like ashes than the fire, but she hadn't felt like this in years.

Shit. She couldn't remember a kiss *ever* making her this wet. It wasn't the kiss itself that drove her crazy, but all those months of anticipation. All those moments she'd spent with him, wishing one of them would be strong enough to tell the other how they felt. Waiting for him had created this snowball of passion that had been slowly building, forming, and growing since she'd met him. Now, finally being in his arms was like sunshine after a hurricane. Like the first drop of rain after months of wildfires and drought.

"Oh." Wesley gyrated on top of her, pumping and sweating as the heat from the fire blanketed their naked bodies.

All this time, she wondered how she'd keep fighting him. How she'd stop herself from falling under his spell. Now she understood.

She could fight him until eternity, but she couldn't fight her own heart.

So finally it was here. The showdown. She and him rolling around on nature's pallet while they succumbed to ecstasy she'd long forgotten.

"I love you, Chanel." He thrust deeper inside of her, their bodies slipping against each other from humid sweat. "I've always loved you."

She wrapped her arms around his shoulders, riding the waves of uncertainty and passion wherever he wanted to take her.

CHAPTER THIRTEEN

Despite being in Alex's warm arms, Aria shivered in the backseat of the forest ranger's truck, not from being cold, but from the fear of never seeing her mother again. She'd tried to be strong and not panic, but Chanel was her entire world. All she could think about was living without her. How would she go on without her best friend and mother, the most important person in her life?

Aria gave up pretending to be strong. She broke into tears, laying her head on Alex's chest.

"It's okay." He rocked her. "You can't think negatively."

Within 30 minutes of Aria finding out what happened, Eddie, the forest ranger and Sam had comprised a small search party including the hikers Chanel and Wesley had gone with, some random guests from the resort, and a few of the resort's security guards. They'd been out there at least an hour, setting up parameters and searching as best they could at night. But despite Sam and Eddie's expertise in the wilderness, Aria lost hope instead of gaining it.

"I just keep thinking about not seeing her again." Aria sniffled as the glimmer from various flashlights flashed across the forest. "How could they disappear?"

"I got lost in the woods once." Alex rubbed the top of his head. "I was about ten and the family went to our cabin in the Colorado mountains for Christmas. I wandered away but you know what kept me hopeful?"

"What?"

"Remembering that I had someone waiting for me who loved me. Someone looking for me. I was only out there for a few hours, but being a kid, it seemed like an eternity. Your mother wouldn't want you worrying, Aria. Your mom wants you to be strong."

"She's my best friend." She touched the pendant on her necklace. "I can't live

96

without her, Alex. I can't."

He sat up. "Here comes Eddie."

Aria sprung up and opened the back door. "Did you find them?"

Eddie sighed, shaking his head. "But don't worry, okay? There's a lot of ground to cover and we're gonna stay out here all night if we have to."

"Why the hell do you guys keep telling me not to worry?" Aria bounced. "This is my mother we're talking about! I'm sure you're more concerned with finding Mr. Babcock, but she's important too!"

"Aria." Alex took her hand. "That's not fair."

"That's what it seems like to me."

"Miss Adeyami, I assure you we want to find them both." Eddie pulled up his pants, his oversized ranger hat slipping down his narrow forehead. "You can have trust in me all right? I know this forest better than anyone except maybe Sam, so if they're out here, we'll find them."

"What if they're *not*?" Aria griped. "Huh? What if some animal got to them?"

"Animals don't approach people," Eddie said. "That's a myth. Bears, coyotes, they will do all they can to stay away from humans, and I'm sure Mr. Babcock has prepared himself for them to be safe."

"This is terrible." Aria sobbed. "It's my fault."

"How is it *your* fault?" Alex asked.

"I pushed her to go! She wanted to spend time with me today and as always, I was too selfish to. Now she's gone."

"Have you tried calling her again?" Eddie asked.

Aria frowned. "No signal, remember?"

"Look, it's doing no good for you two to be here," Eddie said. "Why don't you go back to your cabin and rest?"

"Don't dismiss me like I'm some little kid," Aria said. "I'm not going any damn where until my momma comes walking out of that forest and if you can't find her, then get my wheelchair and I will!"

Eddie held his waist. "I don't think that's a good idea."

"Then find her!" Aria pointed toward the terrain. "Instead of wasting time telling *me* what to do."

"Okay, you can stay. Are you guys hungry or anything?"

Aria scoffed as Alex shook his head.

"We have plenty of food if you need it." Eddie turned on his flashlight. "We'll find her, Aria. I promise."

****

Chanel giggled as Wesley nibbled on her fingertips.

"Your hand's so small. I bet I can put your whole fist in my mouth. Look." He spread his lips wide and tried to swallow her hand.

"Ha, ha, ha!" Chanel laughed, swatting at his cheek. "You're so silly. If all those high society business folks could see you now, huh?"

Buck naked, they snuggled together in Wesley's double sleeping bag.

"I must ask." Chanel caressed his pecs. "Was your plan to seduce me all along when you barged in on the hike?"

"Well, the way I look at it is you seduced *me*." He kissed her forehead. "You've been seducing me since we met."

"Really? How do you figure that?"

"That first day when you arrived for work..." He raised his eyebrows. "I was in

awe of you. Not just your beauty, though that blue-gray pantsuit hugged your body oh so well." He cackled.

She grinned. "You remember what I had on?"

"I always remember what you have on. But your beauty is only half of it. You impressed me with your spunk. I loved how you walked right up to me with your plans to redo all the books. Of course, I'm thinking you're crazy but you showed *me*, didn't you?" He pushed his fingers through her curls. "The best damn accountant I've ever had."

"When did you realize you were in love with me?"

He swatted a gnat off his cheek. "The first day. Then my plan sprang into action. Had to do a lot of manufacturing to be alone with you."

"What do you mean?"

He snickered. "I don't reveal my evil plans, but all those times we 'worked' late? That stuff could've waited until the morning. I just wanted an excuse to be with you."

"I had a feeling." She smiled, tangling her legs in his. "And every time you called, I came running without a fight. That's when I knew I was in love with you, too."

Wesley smiled so widely he showed teeth.

"It's funny." Chanel rubbed his shoulder, loving how she could just touch him whenever she wanted without feeling awkward about it. "We spend our lives wanting to control everything but we couldn't control this. Couldn't control how we felt."

"It's true what they say. Can't control your heart." He kissed her, holding her to his warmth. "I meant what I said, Chanel. I love you."

"Wesley—"

"You don't have to say it back." He smiled. "At least not yet. I just want you to
know how I feel."

"Are you sure about all this? Me and you?"

"I know I don't wanna go another day without you being with me for every step I take from now on."

"I come with a lot of baggage." Chanel stroked Wesley's cheek. "I have a daughter, and I'm not from your world, Wesley."

"What do you mean?" He scoffed. "You belong in my world more than I do. That's what I love about you. Plus, it's not 'my' world. It's 'our' world." He kissed her. "And I'm gonna be the best stepdad I can be."

"Stepdad? Hold your horses, son." Chanel coughed between laughing. "Let's see how this dating thing works first. You know how we get on each other's nerves. We'll probably kill ourselves on the first date."

He pressed his erection against her thigh. "There's only one way you could kill me and I can't think of a better way to die."

She laughed as she brought his face into hers for another kiss.

"Hello?" a man's voice yelled.

"You heard that?" Chanel let Wesley go. "Is someone out there?"

"Hello?" the man yelled again. "Mr. Babcock? Miss Adeyami? Are you out here?"

"Oh!" Chanel shrieked. "Yes!" She swatted Wesley with excitement. "We're over here, uh, by these rocks and stuff! Wesley, they found us!" She hugged him. "Ah! Thank you, Jesus." She unzipped the bag and grabbed her clothes, but Wesley just sat there with his face dragging the ground. "Come on, get dressed. What's wrong?"

"Maybe I don't wanna leave. Because if we leave, maybe things will go back to how they were. You running again."

"I'm not going anywhere." She lifted his chin and kissed him. "We're together,

Wesley. Nothing's gonna change that."

He smiled as the sparkle of a flashlight bounced off the rocks from the opposite direction.

"Hello?" the man called out again.

"That's Eddie," Wesley said. "He's the forest ranger. Eddie, we're behind the rocks! Come on!"

"Wait, hold on, Eddie!" Chanel struggled to get dressed. "Wait right there!"

"Huh?" he asked. "Are you all right?"

Chanel and Wesley laughed as they hurried to dress.

"Just a second!" Wesley said. "We're just... just give us a moment."

"What in the world?" Eddie groaned.

Chanel and Wesley fell over on the ground, half-dressed and laughing.

****

"Momma!"

"Aria!" Chanel broke from Wesley's embrace and raced to the ranger's jeep and grabbed Aria into a tight hug. "Oh, baby. I missed you."

"Mom, I was so scared." Aria hung out the backseat. "I thought you might be dead!"

"No, honey." Chanel kissed Aria's cheeks and held her face in place so she could look at her. "I'm never leaving you and I told you that."

Aria held out Chanel's hands, examining her. "Are you sure you're okay?"

"I'm fine, sweetie."

"What happened?" Aria asked.

"Well, we weren't paying attention to the group." Wesley shrugged. "Got separated and before you knew it, we were walking around in circles. Hey, Alex."

Alex waved. "Hi, Mr. Babcock."

"Oh." Aria giggled, pulling Alex's shirt. "Momma, this is Alex Stepford. Alex, this is my mother Chanel."

Alex extended his arm from behind Aria. "Hello, Miss Adeyami. It's nice to meet you. Happy Memorial Day."

"Jeez," Wesley said. "I forgot. This *is* Memorial Day, huh?"

Taken aback at just how gorgeous Alex actually was, Chanel gave a sly wink to her blushing daughter as she took the young man's hand. "Nice to meet you too, Alex. Heard a lot about you."

"You too." He put his arm around Aria.

"Momma, if it weren't for Alex, I'd have gone crazy." Aria took his hand. "He talked me off the ledge."

"I appreciate that, Alex." Chanel smiled at him. "Aria, this is Wesley Babcock."

Wesley's dimples sprouted as he took Aria's hand and kissed it. "Charmed. And may I say you're just as lovely as your pictures?"

Aria giggled. "Well, I guess it's true what they say about you. You *are* smooth."

Chanel grabbed Wesley's hand. "Guess Wesley talked *me* off the ledge as well."

Aria's eyes sparkled, signaling she got Chanel's hint that she and Wesley were now together. "Thank you for looking after my mother, Mr. Babcock."

"Oh, let's not get it twisted," he said.

Chanel gawked at him.

Aria laughed. "I see you've been spending a lot of time with Momma because that's one of her favorite phrases."

"Don't credit me for anything." Wesley beamed. "Chanel is more than capable of taking care of herself. I was just along for the ride."

"No, no." Chanel stuck her finger in the air. "You kept me grounded, Wesley. That bridge. Woo."

"What bridge?" Alex asked.

"Wesley fell through it and almost died."

The teens gasped.

"We were walking around in circles," Chanel said. "Felt like that episode of *The Twilight Zone* when that couple kept driving around the same area over and over."

"Were you scared?" Aria asked.

"A little." Chanel smiled up at Wesley. "But Wesley has a way of making you comfortable."

"Actually, we spent most of the time fighting." He laughed. "It took our minds off being lost."

"I'm so happy." Aria hugged Chanel again. "If anything happened to you I don't know what I'd do."

"You'd have survived." Chanel patted her back. "Just like I taught you how to."

Wesley gestured at Alex. "Have you ever met two stronger women?"

Alex's eyes sparkled. "No."

Eddie and Sam approached as the rest of the search party meandered toward their cars but not before giving warm thoughts and greetings to Wesley and Chanel for making it back.

"Woo." Sam grinned, waving his baseball cap. "You two gave us quite a scare. I'm glad you're all right."

"Thanks, Sam." Chanel hugged him. "If it weren't for you acting so fast and getting Eddie, we could've been out there for God knows how long."

"Never underestimate nature." He pointed toward the hills that glowed in the
moonlight. "The wilderness is tough and a lot of bad things can happen if you're not careful."

Wesley drank from the water bottle Eddie had given him. "When did you notice we were missing from the group?"

"Immediately." Sam grinned. "The way you two were bickering, it was impossible to ignore. So we looked all around and when we didn't see you, I came back to the resort and called Eddie."

"Looks like my money's well spent." Wesley touched Sam's shoulder. "It's nice to know my guests are in good hands if this happened again."

"Mr. Babcock almost fell off a bridge," Aria said.

"Yeah, that bridge." Sam nodded. "Gosh, you guys were nowhere near us then. We didn't even go in that direction."

"Anything else you folks need?" Eddie asked. "You guys ready to go back to the resort?"

"Hold on a second." Wesley squeezed Chanel's hand. "Give us a minute, would you?" He pulled Chanel from the group. "You okay?"

"I'm *fine*." She pushed up against him. "I just hope Aria's exhausted tonight."

"Why?"

Chanel French-kissed him. "Why do you think?"

"Ah, so she can be asleep and we can have some fun." He pulled on her curls. "You did a hell of a job raising her. She's a wonderful young lady."

"Yeah." Chanel looked back at her daughter who had her head on Alex's shoulder as he comforted her. "She's growing up and I have to face it. Soon, she won't need me as much as she used to. I'm glad about that but scared at the same."

"She's gonna always need her mother. Look at how upset she was when we were

missing." Wesley cuddled Chanel. "Besides, you'll be too busy thinking about *me* to worry about Aria."

"Really?" She laughed as he kissed her. "You think so, huh?"

"I know so. It's a new world, Miss Adeyami. Are you ready for what's in store?"

"Oh, you better believe it, Mr. Babcock." She put her arms around his shoulders. "So give me everything you got."

"I plan to." Wesley kissed Chanel's forehead as he rocked her in his arms. "For the rest of our lives."

THE END

To receive book announcements subscribe to Stacy's mailing list:

Mailing List[1]

---

1.   https://stacybooks.eo.page/cjjy6

Don't miss out!

Visit the website below and you can sign up to receive emails whenever Stacy-Deanne publishes a new book. There's no charge and no obligation.

https://books2read.com/r/B-A-RTFC-BPNZB

BOOKS 2 READ

Connecting independent readers to independent writers.

Also by Stacy-Deanne

Billionaires For Black Girls
Billionaire in the Caribbean

Stripped Romantic Suspense Series
Stripped
Captured
Damaged
Haunted
Possessed
Destined
Stripped Series (Books 1-5)

Tate Valley Romantic Suspense Series
Now or Never
Now or Never
Chasing Forever
Chasing Forever
Sinner's Paradise
Sinner's Paradise
Last Dance

Last Dance

The Bruised Series
Bruised
Captivated
Disturbed
Entangled
Twisted

The Good Girls and Bad Boys Series
Who's That Girl?
You Know My Name
Hate the Game

Standalone
The Seventh District
Gonna Make You Mine
Empty
Gonna Make You Mine
Protecting Her Lover
What Grows in the Garden
Love is a Crime
On the Way to Heaven
Open Your Heart
Open Your Heart
A Matter of Time
Hero
Outside Woman

The Watchers
Harm a Fly
Harm a Fly
An Unexpected Love
You're the One
Worth the Risk
Hawaii Christmas Baby
The Best Christmas Ever
Prey
The Good Girls and Bad Boys Series
Bruised Complete Series
Tate Valley Complete Series
The Princess and the Thief
The Little Girl
The Stranger
Oleander
Seducing Her Father's Enemy
Love & Murder: 3-Book Romantic Suspense Starter Set
Paradise
Stalked by the Quarterback
Stripped Complete Series
Tell Me You Love Me
Off the Grid
Sex in Kenya
Fatal Deception
Billionaires for Black Girls Set (1-4)
Theodore's Ring
Wrangle Me, Cowboy
The Billionaire's Slave
Everwood County Plantation
The Lonely Hearts of San Sity
Stranded with Billionaire Grumpy Pants

CPSIA information can be obtained
at www.ICGtesting.com
Printed in the USA
BVHW080830231222
654916BV00005B/124

9 798201 955250